Jacob Finn and the Witching Hour

A Mystery

Margaret S. Baker

Penny Ritchey

ISBN: 1534679766
ISBN 13: 9781534679764
Library of Congress Control Number: 2016909897
CreateSpace Independent Publishing Platform
North Charleston, South Carolina

For my loving family and dear friends, especially Jill Hess and Linda Gray.

And for the wonderful students, teachers and staff at Myers Elementary in Bellwood, PA.

And for a sweet, beautiful girl named Madison Shura.

Chapter One

13-year-old Jacob Finn glanced up at the clock on the classroom wall. It was 3:13 pm.

Two more minutes until the final bell, he said to himself, looking back down at the open paperback copy of *Macbeth* in his hands. It was one of William Shakespeare's classic plays, and Jake (the name most people called him except strangers and his Grandma Finn) tried to pay attention as his eighth grade English teacher, Mrs. Danish, talked about dark supernatural forces, and the consequences of choosing evil over good.

"Did the evil witches actually predict Macbeth's fate?" She asked the class, sitting on the front edge of her desk like cool teachers did. "Or was he so influenced by their predictions that he made them come true? Something to think about, right?" There was a grin on her face, as she posed the question to them. Mrs. Danish always grinned like that when she asked rhetorical questions, or questions that you're supposed to think about but not really answer.

Jake looked at his wrist watch- a gift from his friend, Emily. Then he stared back up at the wall clock. Both showed that there was still a minute to go. Anxious, he squirmed in his seat and buried his nose back in his book, pretending to focus on *Macbeth*.

Normally, he would have been completely wrapped up in that lesson and not counting the minutes at all. Jake loved everything about the supernatural and solving mysteries, and *Macbeth* was full of that kind of thing, but today he was distracted by another mystery. Just before that period, he had found a strange note in his locker.

At first, Jake had thought it was his neighbor and best friend since preschool, Leo Holloway, playing a joke on him. Leo, the class clown, was always doing crazy things like that. But when Jake had stopped by Leo's locker, which was not far from his own, and told him that he had not been fooled, Leo had looked genuinely surprised and had sworn on his guinea pig's life that he knew nothing about it. And since Jake was certain that Leo would never tell a lie with Pork Chop's life hanging in the balance, he had no choice but to believe him.

Finally, the bell rang, signaling the end of the school day and the beginning of a long weekend, since the teachers had meetings on Monday, and the kids were off school.

Jake leapt from his seat and moved swiftly into the hall. He rushed past his locker without stopping. His jacket and books were already in his backpack, and there was no time to hang out in the hall with Leo and talk about their weekend plans, like they usually did on Fridays. Jake had to get to the public library as fast as he could. If the note he had found was real, then Ava Pantloni, the captain of the cheerleading squad and popular girl in the eighth grade, was meeting him there.

As Jake exited the main doors of Grove City Junior High, he was greeted by a chilly October wind. He put on his jacket and then plucked the mysterious note from the side pouch of his backpack and read her words again.

Dear Jake,

I really need your help. Please meet me in front of the library after school. If you don't, something bad might happen to me.

Ava Pantloni

Chapter Two

Jake quickly rode his black BMX dirt bike the three blocks to the library. As soon as he steered into the parking lot, he spotted Ava Pantloni sitting on a bench by the door. It looked like she was texting on her cell phone, and Jake was worried again that it was all some sort of joke. After all, it was only one week before Halloween- the time of year when he knew that people liked to pull pranks.

She was probably messaging Lexi Newberry and Ellis Miller right now, he thought. Telling her best friends about the big joke she was playing on him. Although Jake was a popular kid, he knew that he could still be the target of a prank, especially by a girl. They were unpredictable like that. One minute they were super sweet to you, and the next minute they were laughing at you- something Leo knew all too well after his mom accidentally packed his sister's ***I LOVE BEING A GIRL!*** t- shirt in his gym bag the previous year.

Ava and her friends had giggled about his fashion blunder for weeks afterward, and Jake knew that it had really annoyed Leo, even though he would never have admitted it. Instead, Leo had bragged how the glittery and snug-fitting t- shirt had been such a distraction to the opposing team that each one of them had been picked-off with ease in a gym class dodge ball victory that was sure to go down in the Grove City Junior High record books.

Jake was still straddling his bike, debating whether he should stay or go, when Ava looked up from her phone and noticed him. She immediately stood up and waved.

Even from far away, he thought she looked nervous. She kept looking around and fidgeting with the strap on her bright pink book bag. Now that she had seen him, there was no turning back. He removed his dirt bike helmet (the ones made for bicycles had always seemed so goofy-looking to him) and ran his hand over his short brown hair to make sure it wasn't sticking up. Then he secured his helmet to his bike and locked it to the nearest rack. Finally, he slung his backpack over his shoulder and walked over and said hi.

"Thanks for meeting me, Jake," she said. There was a worried expression on her face, but she still looked pretty, he thought. She had large green eyes and a button nose.

Her long dark hair fell over her shoulders, except for a single braid that swept just above her forehead. The one braid thing was becoming a popular trend with the girls at school, and it was probably because of Ava, he thought. She was the kind of girl that other girls wanted to be like, and Jake had a feeling that she knew it, too. "I didn't know who else to turn to...I mean, you're so good at figuring things out."

"Well, I hope I can help," Jake said modestly, still not comfortable with the reputation he had recently earned after solving a ghostly mystery involving a local historic mansion. Some people said that he was like a kid version of the great fictional detective, Sherlock Holmes, Jake's all-time favorite literary character. But Jake didn't believe the hype. In his mind, he was just an average kid who loved sports, video games and hanging out with his friends, and who couldn't even solve the mystery of why his mom and dad wouldn't buy him a cell phone. Ava Pantloni obviously didn't have that problem.

"You just *have* to help me," she said, sounding desperate. "But we can't stay out here...it's too dangerous. I know she's watching us." Ava looked around nervously. Then she grabbed her book bag and started for the door.

"Wait!" Jake said. "*Who's* watching us?" He scanned the area but saw no one except a pair of joggers pass by. When he turned back around, however, Ava had already entered the library, so he quickly followed her inside.

Chapter Three

Ava led Jake to the only area in the library, other than the circulation desk, where people could talk without getting hushed by Mrs. Foley, the librarian. The zoo room, as the kids called it, was a sound-proof room tucked in the rear corner of the library. Full of long wooden tables and sturdy chairs, it was intended for group school assignments or tutoring sessions. But more often than not, kids would meet up there just to hang out, and the room would get rather noisy, earning its name.

But it was a Friday afternoon, when school work, or even pretending to do school work, was often the last thing on anyone's mind, so that day, the zoo room was strangely quiet.

"I need to ask you something," Ava said, leaning in toward Jake, who had taken a seat across from her. "Do you believe in witchcraft?"

It seemed like a silly question to Jake, but Ava's expression was deadly serious.

"I'm not sure," he said. "Maybe, I guess... I don't know much about that kind of thing. But we've been reading Macbeth in English class, and there's a lot of witchcraft in that, so I guess Shakespeare believed in it."

"Yeah, I know," she said. "I have English with Mrs. Danish right before you."

"Oh, really?" Jake said, pretending it was news to him. She was in the same English class as Leo, and he was always talking about her to Jake and making fun of the questions that she asked in class. He would imitate her voice and say silly things like, "Um, like, Mrs. Danish...do you think Shakespeare ever had explosive diarrhea or picked his nose?" It was hilarious. Leo had always been great at doing impersonations. Not that Jake actually believed that Ava really asked those kinds of questions. He knew that she was a good student, and that Leo was just understandably holding a grudge about the t- shirt incident.

"Yeah," Ava said. "It was actually that class that made me kind of curious about witchcraft. I even bought a couple of books about it from Brumbaugh's Bookstore."

Brumbaugh's was Jake's favorite bookstore. That's where he had bought all of his mystery books, including the ones by Sir Arthur Conan Doyle, the famous author who had created the Sherlock Holmes character.

"I thought we could have some fun with them at my slumber party last Friday night," Ava continued. "Maybe try out some of the spells. But Ellis brought her *Séances and Spells- Girls Just Wanna Be Scared* book, so we mostly used that one because it had instructions on how to play slumber party games, like *Light as a Feather, Stiff as a Board*."

"What's *Light as a Feather, Stiff as a Board*?" Jake asked.

"It's a game where someone lies down on the floor, face up, with their arms tight at their sides and their legs close together, like a toothpick," she said. "Then everyone kneels around them and puts two fingers from each hand under them and starts chanting, 'Light as a feather, stiff as a board,' until you lift them off the ground."

It sounded far-fetched to Jake. "Does it work?" He asked.

"It did for us," Ava said. "But I got so freaked out when I realized that I was a couple of feet in the air that I told them to put me down. It must have broken their concentration because I hit the ground kind of hard. After that, we started watching a movie. We didn't do any witchcraft or anything from those books, so it had to be that stupid game that caused this!"

"Caused what?" Jake said. He still had no idea how Ava was in danger.

"Cause some sort of spell or curse or something...I don't know exactly." Despite the fact that they were alone, she leaned in closer and lowered her voice. "But ever since that night, really strange things have been happening."

Chapter Four

Ava told Jake that the day after her slumber party, a woman with a creepy voice had called her house and had accused her of having something called *the witching hour*, saying that it belonged to her and that she wanted it back. She had told Ava to bring it to Park View Cemetery after dark and leave it on the bench by the angel statue. When Ava had tried to tell her that she didn't know what she was talking about, the woman had become angry, saying that she had put a spell on Ava, and that if she didn't return *the witching hour* by Saturday night then bad things would happen to her.

Jake looked skeptical. "And you think that this has something to do with you playing *Light as a Feather*?" He asked.

"I don't know what to think," she replied.

"And you're sure that you didn't try any spells in the other books?"

"I'm sure," she said. "I didn't try a single one. But I know that *the witching hour* means midnight...I looked it up online. But how do I give someone midnight? It doesn't make sense."

"Well, you're right about what it means," Jake said. "*The witching hour* does mean midnight. It's the time of night when supernatural creatures like witches, demons and ghosts are thought to have their most power, and black magic works best. Some people think that 3am is *the witching hour*, but that's *the devil's hour*, which is a totally different thing."

Ava looked at him like he had three heads.

"Not that I know that much about this stuff," he quickly added, sensing he was losing "cool" points. "And why the bench by the angel statue?" He said, more to himself than to Ava. "I wonder why she picked that place?"

"Who knows?" Ava replied. "Maybe because it's in the absolute creepiest section of Park View Cemetery, and that woman sounded *really* creepy. I mean, who would ever go there? And at night?! That's just crazy!"

Jake had to agree. It was one thing to go to Park View Cemetery on a bright, sunny day with his Grandpa Finn, or Pop, as Jake called him, and visit the graves of Pop's old friends. Jake had done that a lot, and he had never been scared. But hanging out after dark by the large stone angel in the middle of the oldest section of Park View was a totally different thing. Jake figured that a nighttime visit there was like taking a stick to a bees' nest on a summer day. A lot of screaming and running for no good reason.

Ava continued. "And because I didn't go there and give her *the witching hour* back...whatever *that* is," she said, putting her palms up and shaking her head, "bad things really ARE happening!"

"Like what exactly?" Jake asked.

"Well, for starters, I think she's following me," Ava said. "And I keep seeing this stray black cat. And I've been feeling so dizzy lately. I almost fell off the top of the cheerleading pyramid yesterday. Then today, I found these in my locker." She handed him a small black ceramic cat and a crumpled note that read:

Saturday night

Chapter Five

Jake looked at the note. It was written in black marker on ordinary notebook paper. He laid it down and picked up the ceramic cat. With painted eyes, whiskers and a big grin, it looked kind of sweet to him- not at all like the scary black cat images of Halloween. He set it down and picked up the note again. When he turned the paper over, he noticed a dark smudge, like a smeared fingerprint, in the bottom corner. Curious, he ran his finger over a small portion of it. "Did you make this mark when you were holding it?" Jake asked.

"No, it was there. I just figured it was from the marker."

"It's not from a marker," he said. "You see how it got on my finger?" He held up his finger to show her. "Markers dry fast but this is still oily, which means that it's makeup or paint and not permanent marker. Where in your locker did you find this stuff?"

"The note was on the floor, on top of my sneakers," Ava said. "And the cat was on the top shelf."

"Was it locked?"

"My locker?" She thought for a second. "Yeah, I'm sure it was."

"Does anyone else have the combination?"

"No. I don't think so."

"Not even Lexi or Ellis?" Jake asked. Leo had the combination to Jake's locker, just in case Jake was sick and needed Leo to bring a textbook or something home for him, so he figured that Ava might do the same with her best friends.

"No...no one has it but me."

An idea suddenly came to him, and he reached into his book bag and pulled out the note that Ava had left in his locker. "How did you get this into my locker?" He asked.

"I slid it through one of the vents," she said.

"Exactly. And I found your note on the floor of my locker, just like you found this note," he said, holding them both up in the air.

"So?" She said. "I don't get it."

"Why would someone slide a note through the vent, if they could open your locker? We know that they had to open it to put the cat in there."

"I don't know," Ava said. "Maybe she put the cat in there and closed it before she remembered that she wanted to leave a note. So she slipped it through the vent after the door was shut."

"Maybe," Jake said, not convinced. "But it's more likely that the cat and the note were left by two different people. And the person who left the cat was obviously able to open your locker."

"So there are two people out to get me!" Ava exclaimed.

"I'm not sure that anyone's out to get you," Jake said, truthfully.

"Well, I'm pretty sure that there's a witch out to get me...and that she used some kind of magic to open my locker."

Jake thought about Sherlock Holmes' most important rule to solving a mystery: *that once you eliminate the*

impossible, whatever remains, no matter how impr
must be the truth. Jake found it hard to believe that it was possible for anyone to magically open a locker, even a wicked witch.

"The school office keeps the locker combinations on file," he said. "Remember the forms we filled out at the beginning of the school year? Maybe someone got it from there."

"Oh, yeah!" Ava exclaimed. "But how did the witch get into school office without being seen?"

"We don't know that she did," Jake said. "We don't even know that it's a *she* who did it. Someone just might be playing a joke on you." He thought about what he had told himself earlier- people liked to pull pranks that time of year.

"But what about the phone call?! And her threats?! And almost falling off the pyramid?!" She exclaimed. "You sound like my dad...he never believes me either."

Ava's eyes filled with tears, and she began to sob.

"I'm sorry, Ava. That's not what I meant." Jake handed her a tissue from the pack of Kleenexes his mom always stuffed into his book bag even though he had told her a million times that boys don't carry packs of tissues. "I *do* believe you. It's just that things aren't always how they seem at first, and I'm sure you're wrong about your dad."

Ava's father, Edward Pantloni, was a well-respected attorney and the Grove City prosecutor, which meant that he was responsible for proving that someone committed a crime and was punished for it. He was also a very nice man, Jake thought, even though he often seemed sad. Ava's mother had died in a car accident when Ava was only a few months old, and Mr. Pantloni had probably never gotten over it, or at least that's what Jake figured since he had never remarried.

Ava shook her head. "No, I'm not," she said, dabbing away tears. "He's always too busy with work to spend time with me. He doesn't even know my friends. Anyway, he would say that it's just my imagination because I was reading those witchcraft books. Just like when I told him that I thought that Coach Phillips was in the mafia."

"You mean Coach Phillips from school?"

"Yeah," she said. "I saw him behind the Splinters Bowling Alley last week. He was arguing with some guy about money. They were both dressed funny, wearing suits and hats like mobsters, and he gave me a weird look when he saw me. I tried to tell my dad what had happened, but he just said that people were allowed to wear suits and have arguments, and that I shouldn't always jump to conclusions."

Jake couldn't disagree with that kind of logic. The idea that the junior high basketball coach and social studies teacher was secretly a mobster seemed pretty crazy to him. He wondered if Mr. Pantloni was right, and that Ava had a tendency to let her imagination get the best of her.

Then, suddenly, Jake spotted a woman with long black hair and a flowing black coat watching them through the glass door of the zoo room. He sprang from his seat and made a beeline for the door, but the woman was already gone. He rushed through the library until he reached the circulation desk by the main entrance, but there was no sign of the woman, just Mrs. Foley crouched down on the floor picking up papers.

"Excuse me, Mrs. Foley!" Jake called out. "Did you see a woman dressed in black come by here?!"

"Shhh!" She scolded him, rising to her feet. "You know better than to raise your voice, Jacob Finn. And no, I did not," she said, carefully enunciating each word like she always did and that Leo could imitate perfectly.

By then Ava had caught up to Jake. "What's going on?" She asked, looking confused.

"I saw her," Jake whispered. "A woman in black...she was watching us...just like you said."

Chapter Six

Jake and Ava returned to the zoo room to gather their things and figure out what to do next. They decided to meet up at Brumbaugh's Bookstore at noon the next day to ask the owner, Izzy Brumbaugh, about the meaning behind *the witching hour*. She was a nice, old lady and very smart, especially about supernatural things, so Jake thought she might be able to help them.

When they left the library, it was already getting dark outside, and the temperature had dropped. Ava, who was wearing a sweater but no jacket, shivered several times.

"Here," Jake said, taking off his school jacket and holding it out for her. Made of dark blue wool with white leather sleeves, it displayed the basketball and baseball patches that he had earned the previous year, when he had been one of only three seventh graders to make those eighth grade teams.

"No, that's okay. I don't want you to get cold."

Jake laughed. "I'm fine," he said. "Go ahead, put it on."

"Thank you," she smiled, as she slipped her arms through the sleeves and pulled it up around her.

"You're welcome," Jake said. For a split second, he wondered what it would be like to go steady with the most popular girl in eighth grade. But everyone knew that Ava

Pantloni was going steady with Dustin Kelly, the biggest kid in class and the captain of the Grove City Junior High football team. Besides that, Ava Pantloni didn't give Jake butterflies in his stomach. Only one girl made him feel like that.

Jake pushed his bike alongside of them, as they walked in silence, passing several houses with lit jack-o-lanterns and other spooky Halloween decorations. All of it seemed to make Ava more nervous, but Jake loved the decorations and everything else about fall- the crisp, cool air, the pumpkins, hay bales and cornstalks, and the sound of leaves rustling under his feet when he and his dad would toss the football around in the backyard. His mom called it "sweatshirt season," and it was definitely his second favorite time of year, right behind summer.

As they turned onto Ava's street, Jake thought he heard someone cackling in the distance. He looked at Ava, but she didn't react, so he figured that she hadn't heard it. It was probably just someone's Halloween decoration making a noise, he told himself, deciding that it was best not to mention it. She was already scared enough. When they reached the sidewalk in front of her house, he was relieved to see that the porch lights were on, and a car was in the driveway.

"I'll be right back," Ava hollered, darting toward her house.

A minute later, she returned with three books- the two she had recently bought from Brumbaugh's plus Ellis's book.

"She accidentally left it here, but I know she won't mind you borrowing it," Ava said. "That way you can look through all of them and even check out the game, *Light as a Feather*, that I was telling you about."

Jake thanked her for the books and crammed them into his bag.

"I turned the ringer down on my home phone, just in case that woman tried to call again," she said. "But you can call me on my cell phone. I wrote the number on a piece of scrap paper and put it in Ellis's book." Suddenly, she looked worried. "Do you think we can figure it out in time? I mean, I only have 'til tomorrow night."

Jake gave her a reassuring smile. "Everything's going to be okay," he said.

"I hope you're right," she sighed. "Wait...I almost forgot." She removed his jacket and handed it to him. Then she leaned in and kissed his cheek. "Thank you, Jake," she whispered. "See you tomorrow at noon." With that, she ran back to her house and went inside.

For a few seconds, Jake stood motionless on the sidewalk trying to make heads or tails of what had just happened. Had Ava Pantloni really kissed him? He thought. But it was only on the cheek, and she was just grateful for his help, he told himself. After all, she was going steady with Dustin Kelly. The same Dustin Kelly who was very tall and muscular and probably didn't like his girlfriend going around kissing other guys. Jake decided that he should be more careful with other guys' girlfriends in the future.

He put on his helmet and swung his leg over his bike. Just as he started to pedal, however, he heard more cackling in the distance. But that time it didn't sound like a Halloween decoration, and a chill went down his spine. Could there really be a wicked witch out to get Ava? He wondered, looking over his shoulder. Then he turned back around and began to pedal fast. He wanted to make it home before dark.

Chapter Seven

"Mom! Dad!" Jake yelled, as he entered the house through the garage door. He tossed his shoes and backpack on the floor of the mudroom. He could hear the TV in the living room and the jingle of Chrissy's collar, as she raced to greet him. "Hey, girl," he said, leaning over and rubbing her furry face. The black and white mutt, that was more border collie than anything else, nuzzled him affectionately.

He wiped his hands and grabbed a thick slice of garbage pizza from the pizza box on the kitchen island. Garbage pizza was the specialty of Al's House of Pizza and had every topping imaginable and was Jake's absolute favorite.

"We're in here, Jake!" His mom yelled from the other room.

He peeled off a couple of pieces of pepperoni from his pizza and fed them to Chrissy before grabbing a bottle of water from the fridge and leaving the kitchen.

"Hey, slugger," Sam Finn said when his son entered the room. The easygoing financial adviser was reclined in his oversized leather chair with their big gray cat, Duke, curled up on his lap. With brown hair and hazel eyes, he was an older version of Jake. "Where've you been?" He asked.

"At the library," Jake said, casually. He took a bite of pizza instead of offering any more information.

"Well, I'm glad you're home," his mom, Julie, said. The pretty and slender blonde rose from the couch and kissed her son on the cheek. Her long hair was pulled back in a pony tail, and she was wearing yoga pants and a cozy sweatshirt, which meant that she was finished working for the day. Her successful interior decorating business-something that she had started as a hobby several years ago- now kept her busier than the part-time hours she preferred. "We were starting to worry."

Jake grinned and shrugged his shoulders. "I'm totally okay with you guys getting me a cell phone. I mean...just so you wouldn't have to worry so much. I hear that worrying about your child can really age a person."

"Oh, really?" His mom laughed.

"Nice try, pal, but I think we're okay," added his dad, smiling.

Jake knew it was a hopeless argument. He plopped down next to Chrissy on the carpet and changed the subject. "What are we watching?"

"Channel 10 News," his dad said. "Someone may have spotted Michael Pratt at a gas station several states away from here."

Michael Pratt was a local construction worker who had disappeared a week earlier, right after robbing the Grove City First Century Bank. Wearing a Halloween mask and toting a gun, he had managed to get away with a little more than $75,000 in unmarked bills. But one of the bank tellers had recognized his voice and had told the police who he was, so now Michael Pratt was on the run.

"Do you think they'll catch him?" Jake asked.

"I hope so," his dad replied. "According to the news, he's armed and dangerous."

A recent photograph of a smiling Michael Pratt appeared on the screen; there was a phone number beneath it. The reporter said that police were urging anyone with information on Michael Pratt's whereabouts to call the hotline.

"Oh, that reminds me," his mom said. "Leo called."

Jake leapt to his feet. He had forgotten that Leo had invited him and two other friends to stay overnight. "Is it still okay if I go?" Jake asked.

When his parents agreed, he raced upstairs and packed his duffel bag as fast as he could. Then he went to the mudroom and grabbed the books that Ava had given him. He figured that he would need them that night...as long as the guys didn't mind experimenting with a little witchcraft.

Chapter Eight

As soon as Jake arrived at Leo's house, he went down to the basement rec room, where his three closest friends since preschool were already playing a heated game of pool.

"No fair! No fair!" Cried Zachary Cusson, who they all called Cuss, for short.

"Too bad, so sad," Leo laughed.

"Ooh, I call Jake!" Cuss said when he spotted him coming down the stairs. "Now you're going down, Holloway." A chubby and smug-looking Cuss held out a pool stick for Jake, while Leo shook his head with a smile. His blonde buzz cut looked shorter than usual, so Jake figured that Leo had stopped at the barber shop on his way home from school.

"Keep it down, Cuss," said Ahmil Jones, a tall black kid nicknamed AJ. He was leaning over the table in deep concentration, attempting a tricky corner shot. When he missed, he stood upright and looked at Cuss. "Man, my sister talks less than you do."

Everyone laughed except Cuss. "Whatever, AJ," he said. "A good player doesn't need silence to get the job done. Right, Jake?"

"Sure, Cuss," Jake said, already lining up the stick with the cue ball. With one quick strike, Jake made a nice shot to the side pocket.

"Ooh, yeah, ooh yeah," Cuss taunted.

"Stop annoying me, you knucklehead," Leo said, perfectly impersonating their longtime bus driver, Mr. Twiddy, who hated all kids and probably kicked kittens and puppies for fun. At least that's what kids said about him. Jake was always glad when the weather was nice, and he and Leo could ride their bikes to school.

"Shhh...I need to concentrate," Jake joked, as he attempted another shot. That time, he came up short.

"Sugar!" Cuss exclaimed.

The other boys erupted with laughter.

"Sorry, Cuss," Jake chuckled. He had never been a bad sport like Cuss.

"*Sugar*?!" Leo asked.

"Yeah, you heard me," Cuss said matter-of-factly. The legendary swearer since early childhood, who had been nicknamed Cuss not just because his last name was Cusson but also because of his bad language, had recently begun replacing curse words with silly ones. The guys teased him, but Cuss didn't seem to care. If he didn't clean up his act, then his dad, Reverend Cusson, had threatened to send him back to bible camp...and not just for a week, like he did a few years ago, but for the whole summer.

Just the thought of an entire summer spent wearing yarn necklaces, called warm fuzzies, and watching only G-rated movies with wholesome campers had been enough to scare Cuss straight...at least for a while.

"Maybe you should focus a little less on Ava Pantloni and more on the game," Cuss said.

Jake turned and glared at Leo.

"What?" Leo said, defensively. "They wanted to know why you were late."

"So, when's the wedding, Jake? I think June would be nice," AJ joked.

"Maybe," Jake said, playing along. "I didn't give her a ring yet, but she did wear my jacket."

"Gross!" Leo exclaimed. "Is that what that smell is?! Your jacket?!"

"Ooh, Jake, someone's calling your girl smelly," Cuss giggled.

Jake sniffed at his sleeve. "I don't smell anything except the cherry ChapStick she was wearing when she kissed me."

"What?!" The others exclaimed.

"Yep, but I don't think it's right to talk about it," Jake said, smugly. He loved toying with them.

"Pizza's here," Reilly Holloway announced softly.

Jake whipped his head around and saw Leo's twelve-year-old sister already heading back upstairs, her long, dark hair swishing around her shoulders as she moved.

Had she heard what he had said about Ava kissing him? He wondered, hoping that the answer was no. He wouldn't want the girl he secretly liked thinking he liked someone else. That could be a real disaster.

Jake decided that it was time to stop joking around and tell the guys the truth about Ava Pantloni. And there was something else that he needed to tell them...

Chapter Nine

"You want us to play what?" Leo asked, as the boys sat around the kitchen table, devouring pizza and listening to Jake's story about the spell on Ava.

"Light as A Feather," Jake said, eating pizza for the second time that night. "Ava thinks it's the reason she's cursed, so I need to play the game to prove that she's not."

"I don't care if she thinks she's cursed," Leo said.

"Come on...it's a girl's game, so you'll love it," Jake joked.

They all laughed, even Leo. Ribbing each other like that was what they did. It was a sign of how close they were. "Ahhh...you're so funny, Jake," Leo said. "But there's no way I'm floating anywhere."

"No problem," Jake said. "I'll do it."

An hour later, however, Leo was laying nervously on the floor of his dark bedroom with his friends kneeling around him. "I knew I would get stuck doing this."

"You have to," Cuss said. "AJ and I are too heavy, and we need Jake to tell us what to do."

"But won't I be the one who gets cursed...like Ava?" Leo asked. Jake could tell his best friend was frightened. Fearless in the face of bullies or contact sports, Leo was still a scaredy-cat when it came to anything supernatural.

Jake shook his head. "I really don't think there's a curse or spell on her."

"Then why are we doing this?" Leo asked.

"Just to be sure," Jake said.

"Great...that makes me feel soooo much better," Leo wisecracked.

"I'm telling you...you'll be okay," Jake said.

Leo closed his eyes. "Okay, whatever, but I still think this is stupid. Plus, I smell something bad," he said, wrinkling his nose. "Did someone cut the cheese? I know it was you, Cuss."

"Shut up," Cuss said. "Besides, everyone knows that a rabbit smells his own..."

"Both of you shut up," Jake interrupted. "We all have to take two fingers of each hand and put them underneath Leo, and then start chanting, 'Light as a feather'."

"Can I use my thumbs?" Cuss asked.

"Of course not, you moron," AJ said. "Thumbs aren't fingers."

"Yeah, they are," Cuss said, defensively. "When people ask you how many fingers you have, you don't say four... you say five. If you say four, they think you've lost one in an accident."

"Maybe if you're missing a whole hand, stupid," AJ said. "Who doesn't know they have ten fingers?"

"Both of you, shut up," Leo said. "We're not supposed to be talking."

Jake sighed loudly. "Okay, everyone put two non-thumb fingers from each hand underneath Leo."

"And don't touch my bathing suit area," Leo joked, referring to his private parts.

The boys howled with laughter. "Come on, let's get serious," Jake said. "The book said we're supposed to try lifting him up the first time before we start chanting."

On Jake's count of three, the boys tried to lift Leo off the ground but failed to do so.

"It didn't work. I told you this was stupid," Leo said. He started to get up, but Jake pushed him back down.

"It's not supposed to work until we chant," Jake said to Leo. "That's the whole point. We shouldn't be able to lift you until we say those words at the exact same time."

So, the boys began to chant, "Light as a feather, stiff as a board. Light as a feather stiff as a board." They repeated the words over and over, a little out of sync, unlike the directions in the book. At the same time, they tried to lift Leo off the floor, but once again nothing happened. Then, suddenly, Cuss sprang forward, crashing into Leo's stomach and causing chaos in the room.

"What the beans!" Cuss screamed, as Leo groaned in pain. "Something touched my back!"

Chapter Ten

Jake rushed to the wall and flipped the light switch. All the boys winced at the sudden brightness in the room, especially Leo, who was laying on his side, clutching his stomach. His hamster, Pork Chop, was sitting by his head.

"Nice job, Cuss," Leo said, sarcastically. He sat up and cradled Pork Chop in his hands. "You almost killed a defenseless animal."

"It wasn't my fault!" Cuss exclaimed. "I didn't know it was him on my back! Why is he out of his cage anyway?!"

"I bet he's thinking the same thing about you right now," AJ joked.

"Okay, we're really bad at this," Jake said. "I think we need to bring in someone who knows what they're doing."

"You mean a real witch?" Cuss asked.

Jake rolled his eyes. "No, Cuss. I'm talking about a girl. We need the help of a girl if we're going to do this right."

"Well, I'm not getting in the middle again," Leo said.

A few minutes later, Jake was lying on his back on the floor of Reilly's bedroom, surrounded by his friends, including Reilly. Leo had asked her to help them, and she had agreed to do so and had also suggested that they play the game in her room since it had a lot more floor space.

With Reilly now in charge, they began to chant, in perfect time, "Light as a feather, stiff as a board. Light as a feather, stiff as a board." Suddenly, Jake felt himself being lifted off of the floor. He closed his eyes and tried to relax as he hovered in mid-air for several seconds. Then they lowered him back to the carpet and stopped chanting.

"Oh, Man!" Leo said. "That was crazy!"

"You were like floating!" AJ said to Jake, who was already sitting up.

"Do you feel weird?" Cuss asked. "I think I would feel weird."

Jake shook his head. "No, I feel fine." Then Reilly flipped on the overhead light and everyone squinted. "Except for my eyes," he teased.

"Oh, I'm sorry," she said.

Jake smiled. "That's okay. I'm just joking. Thanks for helping us. It was really nice of you."

She blushed a little, as she pushed her red glasses up higher on her nose. She had gotten contact lenses a few months earlier, so Jake rarely saw her in glasses anymore, but he thought that she looked pretty either way.

"You're welcome," she said. "But you never did tell me why it was so important that you play *Light as a Feather*."

"To help Ava Pantloni," Cuss blurted out.

Jake gave him a dirty look. "She played it last weekend and thinks she might be cursed or something because of it. It's no big deal. I'm just trying to be nice." He was rambling, and he knew it. Lately, Leo's little sister, the girl he had known all of his life, who had openly adored him when they were little kids, now made him nervous.

"Wow, that's weird," Reilly said. "I've played this game a few times at slumber parties, and I don't think anyone has ever gotten cursed from it."

Leo filled her in on what Jake had told them about Ava-the mysterious phone call, the dizziness, the weird things in her locker and the woman in black.

"Geez...that does sound pretty crazy," Reilly said. She looked at Jake "Do you really think a witch put a spell on her?"

"I can't say anything for sure...not yet," Jake said, still not wanting to guess. Just like Sherlock Holmes, Jake wanted to gather facts and come to logical conclusions.

"But that was totally witchcraft!" Cuss exclaimed. "What if you get cursed, too?!"

Jake shrugged his shoulders. "Like Reilly said, lots of people have played that game without getting cursed. I think you guys lifting me off the floor had more to do with concentration than witchcraft. You couldn't lift me until all of you were focusing all of your energy on the same thing at the exact same time."

AJ frowned. "But we lifted you with only our fingers."

"Yeah, but they were probably your middle and index fingers, right?" Jake asked.

Leo looked skeptical. "So?"

"Well, those are the strongest ones on your hand and do most of the lifting anyway," Jake explained.

"So, if it isn't a spell or a curse, then what do you think is going on with Ava? A Halloween prank? That's a pretty mean joke." Reilly said.

Jake knew that Reilly couldn't understand people doing such bad things. She had such a kind heart. It was one of the reasons he liked her so much.

"Maybe," Jake said. "At first, I thought it had to be something like that, but now I'm not so sure."

"So, you don't think it's a joke?" Leo asked.

Jake shrugged his shoulders. "I don't know," he said. "But I just can't shake the feeling that Ava might be in real danger."

Chapter Eleven

The next morning, the boys woke up early and went to basketball practice. All of them, except Cuss, who wasn't on the team and had church choir practice instead. It was something he complained about constantly, but Jake didn't buy it. Cuss had a great singing voice and seemed to love showing it off.

Five minutes into practice, Jake had forgotten all about Ava's curse and was focused completely on basketball. He looked good on the court...they all did. Coach Phillips must of thought so, too, because he praised each one of his players several times.

By the time practice was over, however, Jake remembered that he was meeting Ava afterward. He headed to the locker room with his teammates to get cleaned up but then realized that he had left his water bottle on the bottom row of the bleachers. When he went back for it, he heard Coach Phillips talking on the phone in his office. His voice sounded angry. He was arguing about someone named Rachel needing money.

Jake peeked through the glass in the door and saw Coach Phillips sitting with his back to his messy desk. The coach ran his hand over his short blonde hair. A jumbled key chain was smack in the middle of all the clutter. There had to be at least twenty keys on that chain, Jake thought, certain that one of them was the key to the school office, where the locker combinations were kept.

Jake grabbed his water bottle and sneaked back toward the locker room. Just as he opened the door, however, he heard the sound of Coach Phillips leaving his office. Jake slipped through the door to the locker room, as fast as he could, hoping that the coach hadn't seen him. But what if he had? Jake wondered. Just the thought of it made him nervous.

Twenty-five minutes later, Jake had showered and changed and was on his way to meet Ava at Brumbaugh's Bookstore, but he was still thinking about Coach Phillips and his argument over money. What if Ava was right about him being involved with the mafia, he thought. Maybe she had seen something that day behind the bowling alley, and he was trying to scare her. Jake made a mental note to ask her more about Coach Phillips later, but for now he had to focus on talking to Izzy about *the witching hour*.

When Jake arrived at the store, Izzy was busy with another customer and there was no sign of Ava, so he decided to look around. He saw a display of Jane Austen books, which made him think of Reilly Holloway. She had always shared Jake's love of books, and Jane Austen was her favorite author. It was something he had remembered her telling him a long time ago. He picked up one of the books and was paging through it when someone tapped him on the shoulder. He turned around, expecting to find Ava, but it was Reilly standing there. She was wearing a long purple sweatshirt and dance tights, and her hair was up in a bun. He figured she had just come from ballet class.

"Since when do you like Jane Austen?" She asked smiling.

His cheeks reddened slightly. "Oh, I was just looking around...I thought these were cookbooks," he joked, making her laugh. He noticed a Sherlock Holmes novel tucked under her arm. "And since when do you like Sir Arthur Conan Doyle books?"

It was her turn to look embarrassed. "I don't know exactly, but I hear they're pretty good. Is this a good one?" She held up a copy of *A Study in Scarlet*.

"Yeah, it's a great book, but there's another one that I like better," he said, leading her over to the mystery section. After scanning the bookcase for a minute, he slid a medium-sized hardcover off the shelf and handed it to her.

"*The Hound of the Baskervilles*?"

"Yep, it's my favorite," he said. "But you don't have to get it...the other book is good, too."

"No, I want to get your favorite," Reilly said. "I mean, I'm sure I'll love it, too," she added, shyly. She took the book from his hands and opened it. As she read the summary on the inside jacket, Jake noticed Ava enter the store. Looking pale and dizzy, she stopped to balance herself against a table of books. Jake hurried over to her with Reilly following behind him.

"Are you okay? Here, sit down," Jake said, helping Ava to one of the big cozy chairs that was nearby. She exhaled deeply and started to speak but stopped and looked at Reilly.

"Oh, I really need to get going," Reilly said, apparently picking up on the cue.

"Hope you feel better, Ava," she added with sincerity before leaving them and going to the counter to pay for her book.

With Reilly gone, Ava leaned in close to Jake, her eyes wide with fear. "Oh my gosh," she whispered. "You won't believe what happened last night."

Chapter Twelve

Ava told Jake that she and her dad had been awakened in the middle of the night when their house alarm had sounded. She said that her dad had installed the security system a few years earlier just as a precaution, since he had made a lot of enemies putting criminals behind bars, but that the alarm had never gone off before last night. When the police had arrived minutes later, they had determined that it was the back door that had triggered the alarm. They had said that high winds must have jiggled it, and that there had been no break-in attempt, but Ava didn't believe it.

"What did your dad say about it?" Jake asked. He knew that Mr. Pantloni was a smart man.

Ava rolled her eyes. "Of course he agreed with them. He acted like it was no big deal and sent me back to bed, but I couldn't sleep. I know it wasn't the wind. It was her... she was trying to get me." Ava looked terrified, and Jake quickly decided that it was not the time to mention Coach Phillips, and the conversation he had overheard.

Then he saw Reilly walk out the door with her purchase and noticed that Izzy was no longer busy with customers. She was leaning up against the counter, her nose buried deep in a book. He told Ava that he'd be right back, but her dizzy spell had passed, so she insisted on going, too.

"Excuse me, Mrs. Brumbaugh," Jake said, politely, as he approached the counter.

The white-haired old lady immediately put down her book and stood upright.

"Goodness gracious," she smiled, her crystal blue eyes twinkling behind gold wire- framed glasses that she always referred to as her spectacles. "You know you're supposed to call me Izzy, my dear friend, Jake." She wrapped her tan, wooly, cardigan sweater tighter around her generous-sized waist. "And where have you been these past few weeks? I thought you must have given up reading and had been sucked up into one of those silly video games!"

Jake laughed. "No, not yet," he said. "I've just been kind of busy with school and stuff."

"Very good, very good...and how are you, Miss Ava?"

"Fine, thank you," Ava said, unusually shy.

Izzy plucked a cracker out of her pocket and fed it to her African Gray parrot, named Jasper, who was perched in a large cage behind her. Having a parrot in the store was one of those quirky things that made Brumbaugh's different from a typical bookstore.

"Good girl" Izzy said, as the bird ate hungrily. "Now, what can I do for you two today?"

"Actually, Mrs...I mean, Izzy," Jake said, leaning toward her and keeping his voice low. "We kind of need your help. Can you tell us everything you know about the term *the witching hour*?" He left out the part about the books, and that some crazy lady, who may or may not be a witch, was threatening Ava. He didn't want Izzy to think they had lost their minds.

"Ahhh...*the witching hour*," Izzy grinned mischievously. "The stroke of midnight. That strange sliver of time which marks the end of one day and the beginning of another. When the wall between our world and the supernatural world becomes so thin that spirits can easily slip back through it." Her voice was hypnotic. "Or at least that's what many people think."

"Is it possible to give someone *the witching hour*?" Jake asked.

Izzy paused. "I'm not quite sure what you mean," she said. "But I suppose you can give them the book."

"You mean there's a book called *The Witching Hour*?" Jake asked, excitedly.

"Oh my, yes," Izzy said. "And it's a good one."

Chapter Thirteen

"It was written by Anne Rice, one of my favorite authors," Izzy continued. "I bought a copy from an estate sale about a year ago. It belonged to a woman named Lucinda Storm, who lived just outside of town...until she passed away last year. Now, something tells me that *she* knew a thing or two about *the witching hour.*"

"Witching Hour! Witching Hour!" Jasper squawked loudly, startling Jake and Ava.

"Silly girl," Izzy said to the bird. "Do you want to go in your other cage?" Then she turned to Jake and Ava. "Her birdcage in the storage room is so fancy that she prefers to stay there sometimes, even when I'm not here." She laughed and took a paper cup off the counter and slid it into the cage. "Be careful," she warned Jasper, who was already tearing at the cup, ripping one small piece at a time.

"Izzy, what did you mean about Lucinda Storm knowing about *the witching hour*?" Jake asked, getting back to her story.

"Well, word around Grove City was that Lucinda Storm was a witch."

"Like an actual *wicked* witch?" Ava asked.

"That's what some people thought," Izzy said. "Personally, I never met her, so I'm only going by gossip, but some folks around here were scared of her."

"Why?" Ava asked. "What did she do?"

Izzy folded her arms and leaned back. "I'm not really sure," she said. "I suppose the rumors started because she kept to herself and hardly ever came out of her house. And when she did come out, she always dressed in black and seemed to know everything about everyone...even before they knew it themselves. Some people said that she would turn herself into a black cat and roam the streets at night and that's how she knew everyone's business, but that seemed kind of silly to me."

Ava's jaw dropped. "The black cat," she murmured.

"Do you still have her copy of *The Witching Hour*?" Jake asked.

"I believe I do," she said. "But the story line is rather mature and probably not appropriate for you kids."

"Oh, it's not for us," Jake said. "It's a gift for an adult," he fibbed, feeling a twinge of guilt. He never liked to lie, and he knew that he wasn't very good at it. But Izzy must have believed him because she came out from behind the counter and gestured for them to follow her.

She moved quickly through the store, zigzagging through several tall and full bookcases, until she stopped at a section marked USED FICTION. There she crouched down. "Fiction is arranged in alphabetical order by the author's last name," she said, running her finger over the spines of the books. Then she paused. "Hmmm...it's not here."

She rose to her feet and went over to a cart marked RESERVED, but it wasn't there either. "Let's try the computer," she said.

The three of them went back to the counter, and Izzy quickly rang up a waiting customer before she returned her attention to the search for *The Witching Hour*. Using the keyboard, she carefully typed the letters of the title. After a few seconds, she let out a disappointed sigh.

"What is it?" Jake asked.

"I'm sorry to tell you this, my dears," she said, but *The Witching Hour* is gone."

Chapter Fourteen

"Someone bought it?" Jake asked.

Izzy glanced back down at the screen in front of her. "Yes. Last Friday," she said.

That was the same day that Ava had bought her books, Jake thought.

"One of my employees must have sold it. I took that day off to do a little shopping."

Jake knew both of Izzy's employees. Becca was a cheerful young woman, who also worked at The Doughnut Hole, and Frank was a smart thirty-something, who performed in local theater.

"But I'm sure we can order you another copy," Izzy said. "Hang on. I'll be right back." She left to help a confused-looking shopper before Jake could explain to her that they didn't need to order another book. They needed to find the book that had belonged to Lucinda Storm.

"That's the guy who checked out my books last Friday," Ava said, motioning toward Frank, who had just walked in the door carrying a travel coffee mug. He was headed straight toward them. Jake smiled and said hello.

"Hi," Frank nodded casually, passing them, as he went behind the counter. He took his cell phone out of his pocket and looked at it.

"Ring, ring, ring," Jasper said, sounding just like a telephone.

"Wow!" Jake said. "That's pretty cool."

"It can get a little annoying," Frank said, tucking his phone behind a pile of books on the shelf behind him. "She does that every time she sees a phone. Can I help you guys find something?"

"Izzy thought you might be able to help us," Jake said, fibbing again.

Jasper made a few clicking noises and stared at Jake, as if to scold him.

"Sure thing...what can I do for you?" Frank said, stacking books on the counter.

Ava spoke up. "There's a book called *The Witching Hour*, and it..."

"Witching Hour!" Jasper shrieked, startling Ava.

She gave the bird a dirty look. "And it was sold last Friday," she continued. "Some woman thinks that I bought it, but I didn't, and we were hoping that you would remember who *did* buy it."

Frank stopped what he was doing. "It was probably the same woman who talked to Becca," he said.

"What woman?" Jake asked.

Frank suddenly looked confused. "Wait...*you* didn't buy *The Witching Hour*?"

He was looking at Ava.

"No," Ava insisted. "I don't know anything about that book."

"Then it must have been that other girl who was in here that day," Frank muttered to himself. "She was here around the same time that you were, and you both bought books about witchcraft. I hope that woman isn't bothering you. My co-worker, Becca, said that she seemed really angry."

"Wait a second, Frank," Jake said. "So, a girl bought *The Witching Hour* on Friday, and some woman came in later and asked who had bought it?"

"Yes," he replied.

"And you told her *I* did?!" Ava interrupted.

"No, Becca talked to her, not me," he said, putting his hands up in protest. Then he added, sheepishly. "But I'm the one who told Becca that you bought it."

"Well, because of you, there's some crazy woman after me," Ava said sharply.

Frank lowered his head in shame. "I'm so sorry," he said. "It was a really weird day. Izzy wasn't here, and Becca didn't come in until four o'clock, so I was by myself for most of the day."

"Frank, do you know the name of the other girl...the one you mixed up with Ava?" Jake asked.

"Ummm..." He closed his eyes for a few seconds before they popped back open.

"Nightingale!" He cried out like an excited game show contestant. "Her last name is Nightingale! Does that help?"

"It sure does," Jake said. He looked at Ava and knew that they were thinking the same thing- there was only one girl in town with the last name Nightingale.

Jake thanked Frank, and then he and Ava headed for the door.

"Be careful!" Jasper screeched as the two kids exited the store.

Chapter Fifteen

Jake left his bike chained to the light pole outside of Brumbaugh's, while he and Ava hurried to Mariah Nightingale's house. She was a new classmate of Jake and Ava's, having recently moved to Grove City with her mom, Bettina. They were the only Nightingales in town, and Jake and Ava knew where they lived because most people in Grove City knew where everyone else lived.

"I remember seeing Mariah walking into the store around 3:30 that day...right before I left!" Ava exclaimed. Then her excitement disappeared. "But I'm worried she won't help us. We have gym class together, but we don't really talk much. She reads books in the bleachers while all the other girls swim laps, and I don't think she likes any of us."

"It's worth a shot," Jake said, wondering if it wasn't the other way around and that Ava and her friends hadn't been very nice to Mariah. He knew that she was quiet and artsy and usually wore black, which kind of made her a sitting duck for teasing, although she didn't seem to care much. She sat by herself at lunch, and whenever Jake had asked her to sit at his table, she had just smiled and said no thanks.

Soon, they approached her house- a small white Cape Cod with black shudders and a green door. For years, it had belonged to the Haverly family and had been called the Haverly house. But Mr. and Mrs. Haverly's kids had grown up, and they had sold the house to Mariah's mom and had moved to Florida. And although the Nightingales lived there now, most people still called it the Haverly house. Grove City was slow to change like that.

With Ava standing partially behind him, Jake knocked on the front door, careful not to disturb the seasonal wreath that was hung on it. There was a scarecrow, two jack-o- lanterns and a few other fall decorations arranged attractively by the door. It was apparent to Jake that Mrs. Nightingale had a good eye for decorating and took pride in her modest home.

They waited for several minutes without an answer. Fortunately, Ava had a pen and a small scrap of paper in her purse, so Jake quickly wrote a note, folded it tightly and wedged it into the doorway. He and Ava stepped off the front porch, and Jake looked back at the house before leaving.

"What did you write?" Ava asked, hugging herself tightly for warmth, as they headed back toward Brumbaugh's to get Jake's bike.

"I wrote down my phone number and asked her to call me. I told her that it was really important."

"You didn't mention my name?"

"Nope," Jake said.

Ava sighed with relief. "Well, that's good. I don't think that she would call you if she knew that it had something to do with me."

"I really hope that's not true," he said.

"Why?" Ava asked, stepping over a large crack in the sidewalk.

"Because Mariah Nightingale was watching us from her bedroom window."

Chapter Sixteen

"You saw her?!" Ava exclaimed.

Jake shook his head. "Not exactly. But I saw a pink curtain move in an upstairs window, and there wasn't a car in the driveway."

Ava looked at him like he was speaking a foreign language.

"Pink curtains usually mean it's a girl's room," he explained. "And since the car was gone, Mariah's mom probably wasn't home, so I'm pretty sure that it was Mariah who moved the curtain when she was looking out her bedroom window."

They walked in silence for a few seconds. "You're really smart," Ava said, as they turned onto Main Street.

"No, it's just that I've always been able to focus on small details. My mom says it's a form of OCD."

"What's that?" Ava asked.

"It stands for Obsessive Compulsive Disorder," he said, "which means you have to do things a certain way or else it drives you crazy."

Ava laughed. "I think my dad has that."

Jake began to laugh, too. Then he spotted Reilly Holloway and Dustin Kelly sitting by themselves at a window seat at Al's House of Pizza, and the smile was wiped from his face. Feeling sucker-punched, he picked up his pace and walked quickly past the window, pretending not to see them.

"Are you okay?" Ava asked.

Jake forced a weak smile. "Yeah, just tired from practice, I guess." If Ava hadn't noticed her boyfriend with another girl, then Jake certainly wasn't going to tell her. He figured that she had enough to worry about. But then it occurred to him that maybe Ava and Dustin weren't going steady anymore, so he asked her about it.

"I broke up with him last week," Ava said. "He never had time for me. All he talked about was football this and football that, and I got tired of it. Why do you ask?"

There was a curious smile on her face, and it suddenly occurred to him that she might think that he liked her.

"I was just wondering if he might have a reason to play a mean joke on you," he said, matter-of-factly.

"Oh," she replied, clearly getting the message. "No, not Dustin. He only cares about football. I can't see him pulling a prank or trying to get back at me. He wasn't even that upset when I broke up with him."

They arrived outside of Brumbaugh's, and Jake bent down and untied his bike.

Then he pushed it alongside of them as they walked toward Ava's house. During that time, Jake couldn't help but wonder if Ava was wrong about Dustin. Guys usually liked to play it cool when it came to breakups. They acted like they didn't care even when they did. Maybe Dustin Kelly was secretly angry about Ava breaking up with him and was getting revenge by scaring her. And now he was spending time with Reilly. Was getting Ava jealous part of his plan?

Chapter Seventeen

"So what happens now?" Ava asked, as they stood outside of her house.

"I wait for Mariah to call me," Jake said. "Then I get *The Witching Hour* from her and take it to Park View Cemetery tonight."

Ava looked worried. "That sounds dangerous...and what if she doesn't give it to you?"

"Don't worry," Jake said. "She seems like a really nice girl. I'm sure she'll want to help."

"I don't know," Ava frowned. "If she did buy *The Witching Hour* then maybe she's the one who put a spell on me."

Jake had wondered about that, too, but didn't tell Ava. "Let's not jump to conclusions," he said. Then he reassured her that everything would be okay and told her that he'd call her the next day.

"Okay," Ava sighed. "If I don't pick up, just leave a message. I have cheerleading practice tomorrow afternoon, and I'm going to Lexi's house afterward for a sleepover because my dad has to work late...on a Sunday," she added, rolling her eyes.

Jake felt bad for Ava. Her mom was gone and her dad was always busy with work, and he could tell that she was sad about it. Although they sometimes drove him crazy, Jake felt lucky that his parents and grandparents were always there for him.

Ava wished Jake good luck and went inside. As soon as she closed the door, Jake saw a black cat dart across the yard and disappear into the bushes beside her house. It had to be the same black cat that Ava thought was following her, Jake thought. He remembered what Izzy had said about Lucinda Storm, and the rumors that she had roamed the streets as a black cat. It was a silly thought, he decided. And that black cat was probably just a neighborhood stray.

He swung his leg over his bike and looked back at the area where the cat had disappeared. There was no sign of it anywhere. Then he spotted it sitting on Ava's front porch. It was wearing a light blue collar with a silver tag in front. That meant it belonged to someone, and it wasn't a stray.

Slowly, Jake got off of his bike. He wanted to read the cat's tag. The owner's name and address would be on it. As soon as he took one step toward the cat, however, it sprang off of the porch and ran away. He figured that it was going home, where it would be safe. He decided that he needed to do the same...he didn't want to miss Mariah's phone call.

Chapter Eighteen

Jake made it home in record time. His mom told him that he had missed a phone call, but it had been a call from Leo and not Mariah. He knew what Leo had wanted- to go over their movie plans for that night. They were supposed to go see the horror spoof, *Zombies Don't Wear Skinny Jeans,* but Jake couldn't go after all. He had to help Ava instead. It was the right thing to do, even though he knew that his best friend would be disappointed.

He grabbed some food from the fridge and went to his room. Then he picked up the two-way radio and squeezed the button twice on the side of the device. Two clicks.

Since neither of them had cell phones, that was their long time signal for "Are you there?" But there was no response. He waited a few minutes and tried again. Nothing but static. Leo was probably at his grandma's house, Jake thought. He and Reilly usually went to see her on Saturday afternoons. Jake wondered if Reilly had gone with Leo that day or if she was still with Dustin. He pushed the thought from his head. He had more important things to focus on... like why hadn't Mariah called? He was getting antsy.

He went to his desk and searched the words Lucinda Storm/ Grove City on his laptop computer. Only two things came up: a notice from last October about her estate sale and her obituary. Jake clicked on the obituary. It said that she had died a year ago at the age of 72. No mention of how she had died or what people had thought of her, but it did say that she was survived by a grown niece, named Rachel Storm, who lived in Grove City.

Jake's face lit up. He thought about Coach Phillips' phone conversation- something about Rachel needing money. Was that the same Rachel? He wondered.

Curious, Jake quickly typed Rachel Storm/Grove City and hit enter. A few seconds later, only one search result appeared on the screen- *Rachel Storm buys Splinters Bowling Alley.* The same bowling alley where Ava had spotted Coach Phillips arguing about money with a shady-looking man.

According to the article, Rachel Storm had moved to Grove City after the death of her aunt and had bought the old bowling alley with hopes to improve business. But Jake had heard that it still wasn't doing that well.

He looked at the picture of Rachel Storm that was next to the article. She had short brown hair and dark eyes. Jake tried to picture her wearing a long dark wig. Could Lucinda Storm's niece, Rachel, be working with Coach Phillips to scare Ava? He wondered. Had Ava accidentally witnessed some criminal behavior at the bowling alley and didn't even know it?

Jake quickly found the piece of paper with Ava's number on it. Then raced downstairs, picked up the phone and called her.

Chapter Nineteen

The phone rang several times before going to voicemail. "This is Ava...leave a message! Thanks!" Her recorded voice was super cheerful.

"Hey, Ava, this is Jake. Call me at 555-3885. Bye." Short and sweet. Not like when Gram left messages on their answering machine. She went on and on, as if she was actually talking to someone.

If Gram had left Ava a message, she would have probably said, "Hey, Ava. Do you remember that bowling alley where you saw Coach Phillips arguing about money? Well, apparently, it's owned by the niece of the woman who came back from the dead and is out to get you because she thinks you have her book. Hugs and kisses! Have a great day!"

Grinning at the thought of his sweet Gram's ridiculous phone messages, Jake looked at the clock on the wall. It was 2:13 pm, and Mariah still hadn't called. He was tired of waiting. He took the newest edition of the Grove City phone book out of the kitchen junk drawer and began flipping through the pages. As soon as he found the "N" section, he slid his finger down the list of names. Nielsen, Niemi, Nier, Nightingale.

Bettina Nightingale. Bingo! He thought. That had to be Mariah's mom.

He picked up the phone again and dialed the number. But before it could ring, he changed his mind and hit the end button. He had no idea what he was going to say.

Should I tell Mariah the whole story? Should I mention Ava? What if she thinks it's some sort of Halloween prank? The call was too important to mess up.

Jake thought about the advice that Leo always gave. "Keep it simple, stupid." If you took the first letter of each of those words it spelled KISS. Leo would shout out, "KISS!" whenever anyone was over-analyzing anything in his presence. It meant keep things as simple as possible and not think too much. With that in mind, Jake took a deep breath and dialed Mariah's number again. It rang four times before a girl answered.

"Hi, is this Mariah?" Jake asked.

"Yes, it is," she said, warmly.

Jake cleared his throat. "Hi, Mariah, it's Jake Finn... from school."

"Hi," she said, her tone no longer friendly.

Jake wondered what he had done to make her suddenly not like him. Was it just because she had seen him with Ava? "I'm sorry to bother you," he said. "But I left a note on your front porch..."

"What do you want, Jake?" She cut him off.

Keep it simple, stupid went through his head. "It's kind of a long story, but Brumbaugh's sold you a used book called *The Witching Hour*, and the woman who used to own it wants it back."

In a smart tone she said, "So, why do you care? Do you work at Brumbaugh's?"

"No, I don't," Jake replied. "But like I said, it's kind of a long story. You see, the woman thinks that Ava Pantloni has it, and she's been bothering her about it."

"So why didn't Ava call me? Or Brumbaugh's?"

"Please, Mariah," Jake said. "It's pretty serious. The woman is kind of crazy, and I'm worried for Ava."

"Well, I don't have that book or know anything about it. And if this is some sort of joke, it's not working."

"I swear it's not a joke," Jake said.

But Mariah didn't respond. She had already hung up the phone. Now what do I do? Jake thought, still holding the phone in his hand. Then suddenly it rang.

Chapter Twenty

"Hello?" Jake said, eagerly.

"Hey, why do you sound so weird?" It was Leo. Jake could tell that he was eating something.

"Hi, Leo," Jake said, exhaling deeply. He hadn't realized that he'd been holding his breath. "I thought you were Mariah Nightingale."

"The new girl from school? I had no idea you had a thing for her. Personally, I love her long, red hair, and I probably would have asked her out if..."

"It's not like that," Jake interrupted. "Mariah Nightingale has *The Witching Hour*...even though she won't admit it."

"What do you mean? So you figured out what it is?"

"Yeah, it's a book," he said. "It used to belong to a woman named Lucinda Storm. Mariah bought it from Brumbaugh's the same day that Ava bought her books, but the people who work there made a mistake and told some woman that Ava bought it. So, we stopped by Mariah's house to try to get it, but no one answered. Then I called her but she said she doesn't know anything about it. She thinks we're pulling a prank on her."

"Hmmm," Leo said. "Well, just look up Lucinda Storm's phone number and tell her that Mariah Nightingale has her book. Then she'll leave Ava alone and start bothering Mariah."

"I can't do that," Jake said.

"Why? Because you didn't think of it first?" Leo said, smugly.

Jake could picture his cocky smile. "No, because Lucinda Storm doesn't have a phone. She died last year."

"Seriously?!" Leo exclaimed. "What is it with you and dead people?!"

Jake couldn't help but laugh. "If it makes you feel any better, I don't think it's the dead woman who wants the book."

"Geez...that's great news," Leo wisecracked. "I feel so much better knowing that there's only a slight chance that some dead woman is on the loose."

"Well, I have some bad news, too."

In a glum tone, he asked, "What? We're not going to the movies tonight, are we?"

"I'm sorry, Leo, but Ava's really scared, and I think something bad might happen if I don't help her."

"But how can you help Ava if Mariah won't give you *The Witching Hour*?"

"I might have to use a decoy book."

"What do you mean?" Leo asked.

"It's simple," Jake said. "I'll put a book on the bench tonight in Park View Cemetery and wait to see who takes it. By the time that person realizes that it isn't *The Witching Hour*, I'll have already gotten a good look at them."

"Oh no," Leo grumbled. "Not another cemetery stakeout."

Jake and Leo hadn't been on a stakeout since last summer, when they had hid beside the cemetery of Willow

Mansion, an old, neighborhood house rumored to be haunted. It had been one of the scariest nights of Leo's life.

"Yep," Jake said. "And I'm not leaving there until I see who's behind all of this."

"Correction," Leo sighed. "*We're* not leaving there until *we* see who's behind all of this."

"Thanks, Leo," Jake said. "But I don't think that's a good idea. It might get a little...intense."

"Well, *intense* is my middle name," Leo replied. "Besides, it's not like we're fighting zombies or anything crazy like that. We're just spying on a dead lady who wants her book back." Then he joked, "I mean, how dangerous can that possibly be?"

Chapter Twenty One

So, the boys made a plan. Leo would spend the night at Jake's house, and they would sneak out at midnight and walk the short distance to Park View Cemetery. Once there, they would leave a decoy book on the bench by the angel statue and wait to see who showed up. With his Pro Spy 3000 Night Vision camera, a recent birthday gift from Gram and Pop, Jake would either record exciting paranormal evidence of Lucinda Storm retrieving her book or proof that a real life person had been trying to scare Ava.

At exactly 11:52 PM, the boys stuffed Jake's bunk beds with pillows, just in case one of Jake's parents looked in on them. Then they put on their dark-colored hoodies and crammed their pockets with supplies- a flashlight and snacks in Leo's pouch, and a flashlight and the decoy book in Jake's pouch. Leo had been kind enough to offer up his mom's romance novel, *The Pirate Who Loved Me*, in place of *The Witching Hour*.

After clipping his night vision camera to his belt, Jake turned off the bedroom light and the TV. Then he and Leo headed to the window. It was go time.

Jake went first. With his hood pulled up, he looked like a ninja, as he crawled through the window, expertly securing his footing on the top bar of the two-story trellis. Silently and quickly, he descended to the ground and looked back up at Leo, who was attempting to repeat Jake's tricky maneuvers.

"Don't forget to close the window," Jake said.

"Okay, okay. Don't rush me," Leo replied, clinging nervously to the wooden frame attached to the side of the house. Although he was dressed the same as Jake, Leo looked nothing like a ninja as he nervously shut the window. Moving slowly, he worked his way halfway down before he suddenly lost his balance and fell into the bushes at the base of the trellis.

"I'm okay!" He called out, as Jake rushed over to check on him.

Leo was stuck in the shrub, laying on his back like a helpless turtle. Jake quickly grabbed his arms and pulled him to freedom.

"Man, I thought you were a goner," Jake said, breathing a sigh of relief.

Leo brushed the dirt and leaves from his clothes. "No, I'm great at falling. I'd be an awesome stuntman." He patted the lumpy pouch of his hoodie and removed two bags of candy. "Wait! Where's my spray bottle?!" He exclaimed.

"Shhh!" Jake scolded. The lights were still on in the family room, which meant his parents were still up, and Chrissy was with them. If she heard them, she would start barking. "There it is," Jake said, shining his flashlight on a small white bottle laying beside the shrub.

"Thanks," Leo said, scooping it up. "I feel safer just knowing I have this with me."

"What is it? Holy water?"

"No, Italian salad dressing with extra garlic," he said. "That's way stronger than holy water. You know, all evil entities are afraid of garlic."

Jake laughed and shook his head. “Yeah, I think you told me that before,” he said. He looked back at his house one last time...and then he and Leo headed into the dark night.

Chapter Twenty Two

Like in a scene straight from a horror movie, Jake and Leo entered Park View Cemetery through its large and foreboding wrought iron gates.

"This way," Jake whispered to Leo, as he moved toward the walking path.

They followed its curves in silence as it wound through the cemetery like a dangerous snake. The gas lamp posts that lined it glowed eerily in the darkness, casting creepy shadows all around them. Eventually, the path veered in the wrong direction, and the boys stepped onto a grassy, dark hill full of tombstones. Jake turned on his flashlight and told Leo to do the same.

"Wait," Leo said. "Isn't someone going to see us?"

"That's the idea," Jake replied.

With their flashlights shining brightly, the boys navigated swiftly around every monument and grave marker until they had reached the bench by the angel statue.

Carefully, Jake laid the book down. Then he and Leo walked slowly away from the area, hoping to be seen by the woman in black. Their flashlights lit the way as they headed back toward the path. Then they turned them off and hid behind a large tombstone with a perfect view of the bench.

Jake checked his night vision camera. It was working and ready to go. All he had to do was hit the tiny red RECORD button as soon as something happened. They waited in the dark for several minutes but there was still no sign of anyone.

Suddenly, Leo grabbed Jake's arm. "What was that?" He whispered.

"What was what?" Jake asked.

"I thought I heard something."

They froze like statues and listened. "I don't hear anything," Jake said.

Leo turned and looked behind them. "There it is again... it's like a swishing sound."

When Leo turned back around, Jake grabbed the bag of Whoppers out of Leo's pouch and shook them. "You mean like this?"

"Oh, yeah," Leo laughed. "Sorry."

"Stop goofing around and keep an eye out for someone."

For several minutes, the boys waited in silence. Then Leo tore open his bag of Whoppers and began crunching loudly.

"Keep it down," Jake said. "Someone's going to hear you."

"Shhh...*you* keep it down," Leo snapped. "Besides, you know I eat when I'm nervous." He tossed a Whopper in the air and caught it with his mouth. "Did you see that?" He said, proudly. "Watch, I'll do it again."

Jake shook his head as Leo launched another Whooper into the air. That time, it hit Leo smack in the eye.

"Ow!" He yelped. "I think I'm blind!"

"Shhh! Look!" Jake nudged Leo's arm. A dark figure was headed toward the bench. Jake's pulse quickened. "Here we go," he whispered to Leo. He held up his Pro Spy 3000 Night Vision camera and hit the red RECORD button.

Chapter Twenty Three

The boys watched in silence as a woman with long, dark hair picked up the book and began walking away from the bench. She was slim and average height, just like the woman he had seen at the library.

"I'll be right back," Jake whispered to Leo, as he rose out of hiding, his spy camera still trained on the figure.

Leo yanked on his arm. "No, stay here," he pleaded.

But Jake shook his head and kept moving.

"Then I'm coming, too," Leo said, quickly joining him.

Using the night vision on Jake's spy camera, the boys followed her through a maze of tombstones until she finally disappeared behind a small stone building.

"Is that a chapel or something?" Leo whispered.

"No, it's a mausoleum."

"What the heck is a mausoleum?"

"It's a fancy building with a bunch of tombs inside," Jake said. "Come on. I think she went inside."

"No way," Leo protested.

But Jake was already moving forward. Reluctantly, Leo followed behind him until they had reached the front of the structure, which was marked by two large bronze doors. Jake paused for a second and turned off his camera to save the battery. Then he clipped it to his belt. With

Leo practically clinging to his back, he slowly twisted the doorknobs and pushed inward. The heavy doors opened with a loud creeeeeeek, and Jake heard someone whispering in the darkness.

"Who's there?" He called out, drawing his flashlight faster than a gunslinger. His hand was shaking as he shot beams of light from one dark corner to the next. But there was no sign of anyone, and the whispering had stopped.

"Where'd she go?" Leo asked, turning on his own flashlight to help in the search.

"Are you sure she came in here?"

"I thought she did," Jake said, moving slowly around the room. He counted six large tombs in the middle of the room, each engraved with the last name Stine. And there were two large brass lion heads on the far wall. But no woman in black.

"Man, these are creepy," Leo said, looking at one of the tombs. He took the salad dressing out of his pocket and sprayed both sides of his neck.

Just then, Jake heard the sound of a cat meowing outside of the mausoleum. He turned off his flashlight and told Leo to do the same. Then they tiptoed to the door.

"Wait...why are we spying on a cat?" Leo whispered, straining to see over Jake's shoulder.

"Shhh," Jake said. The strong smell of garlic was making him queasy. He pointed into the distance. "Look over there!"

Chapter Twenty Four

There was a shadowy figure about thirty feet away, heading in the opposite direction.

Jake stepped outside to get a better view. As he reached for his night vision camera, Leo suddenly burst through the doors of the mausoleum, screaming louder and more high-pitched than the entire Grove City Junior High cheerleading squad. Then he tripped and fell to the ground.

"Run, Jake! Run!" Leo shouted, springing back up like a crazy jack in the box.

He took off running, and Jake instinctively did the same, racing behind him until they were safely outside of the cemetery gates.

"What happened?!" Jake asked, panting.

Leo bent over to catch his breath. "There was a ghost in the mausoleum!" He exclaimed. "Or maybe it was a witch! Or a ghost witch! Whatever it was, it walked through the wall and was coming for me!"

"Hold on," Jake said, taking a deep breath. "Now, slow down and tell me everything."

Leo dug in his pouch. "Son of a gun! I lost my salad dressing!"

"Leo, stop messing around and tell me what you saw!"

"I told you!" Leo said. "I saw that creepy lady come right out of the wall with the lion heads!"

"Did she say anything?"

"Yeah, she asked me how I did on my algebra test," Leo wisecracked. "No, she didn't say anything. I took off before we could chat."

Jake rubbed his forehead, thinking about what Leo had told him.

"I'm telling the truth!" Leo insisted.

"I know you are. I'm just working it out in my head. Come on, it's late. Let's go home," Jake said, patting him on the back. He looked down and checked his belt. "Oh, no!" He exclaimed. "My spy camera! It's gone!"

Chapter Twenty Five

The boys made it back safely to Jake's house. But that night, Jake had a bad dream. The woman in black was standing in the middle of the Stine Mausoleum stirring a boiling caldron. Jake could hear Ava screaming for help but couldn't find her anywhere. A black cat was scratching on the outside of the mausoleum door, while the woman in black chanted, "Double, double toil and trouble; fire burn and caldron bubble."

When Jake opened his eyes, it was morning. Beams of sunlight sneaked through his window blinds, highlighting the posters around his room- Michael Jordan, Cal Ripkin, Jr. and Walter Payton. Sports legends frozen in time on his walls. But only one poster caught his attention that morning. It was a fictional drawing of Sherlock Holmes, sitting in his study. His mom had found it at a flea market years ago. He looked at it and then rubbed his eyes, wishing he was as good of a detective as Sherlock Holmes. Soon his thoughts returned to his nightmare.

Double double toil and trouble; fire burn and caldron bubble. He knew those words were from Macbeth. The three witches in the story had said them as a way to make double the trouble for Macbeth. Jake worried that he may have made double the trouble for Ava by leaving the wrong book on the bench, even if his intentions had been good.

Not to mention that his spy camera was gone, and the evidence that he had recorded on it.

Plus, his name and address was on the camera, which might put him in danger.

How could I have been so careless? He thought, staring back at the poster of Sherlock Holmes. He knew that Sherlock would never have made such a stupid mistake.

He caught a whiff of bacon cooking downstairs and his stomach growled. He looked at his alarm clock. It was 9:07 AM. Still tired, he rolled out of bed and noticed that the top bunk was empty. Leo must already be eating breakfast, he thought, suddenly energized to do the same. Quickly, he put on fresh clothes and made a fast pit stop at the bathroom before heading downstairs to join him.

When he walked into the kitchen, however, there was no sign of Leo, just Jake's mom, sitting at the kitchen table, reading the newspaper and sipping her coffee. Chrissy, who had been lying under the table, immediately got up to greet him.

"Hey, girl," Jake said, rubbing the top of her head. She smiled the way dogs do and wagged her tail happily.

"Good Morning, sleepy head," his mom said, setting the paper down. She was wearing jeans and a fleece jacket and her hair was wet. "There's bacon, eggs and toast keeping warm on the stove. Dad went for a quick run and should be back in a few minutes."

"Okay, thanks," Jake said. He grabbed a plate and went to the stove and piled it up with food, while his mom poured him a glass of juice. "Where's Leo?"

"He left a little while ago, but he said to tell you that he would see you at church."

Church services were at noon, but Jake's parents liked to be early, so the Finn's always left the house at 11:30 AM sharp. That didn't leave Jake much time to find his spy camera, shower and change into church clothes. He began eating as fast as he could.

"Geez...slow down, kiddo," his mom laughed.

"Sorry, but I'm kind of in a hurry. I want to take Chrissy for a walk before church."

"That's a good idea...but it's also a good idea for you to chew your food," she joked. Then she took another sip of coffee. "By the way, Ava Pantloni called you this morning." There was a weird grin on her face, which meant that she had it all wrong.

Jake swallowed a mouthful of eggs. "Did she leave a message?" He asked, trying to sound casual.

"Just that she was returning your call from yesterday and that she would call you back this evening," she said, still grinning.

Yep, she definitely had it all wrong, he thought. But he was glad that Ava had called him. He had totally forgotten that he had called her the day before. Now, he had even more to tell her.

"Okay. Thanks," he said, taking his dirty dishes to the sink. Then he went to the key hook by the backdoor and grabbed Chrissy's leash. It made a jingling noise that Chrissy knew all too well, and she ran to him excitedly.

"Don't be too long," his mom said, tilting her head and banging on her ear. "We don't want to be late for church."

Jake gave her a funny look, and his mom noticed.

"No, I'm not crazy," she laughed. "Mrs. Holloway talked me into trying water aerobics this morning, and I forgot my ear plugs." Penny Holloway was Leo and Reilly's mom and one of Julie's Finn's closest friends. "I hope I don't get swimmer's ear again. It always makes me so dizzy."

Jake remembered Ava telling him that she had been swimming in gym class.

Could swimmer's ear be the real cause of her dizziness? He wondered.

Jake slipped his feet into his sneakers and thanked his mom for breakfast. Then he hooked the leash to Chrissy's collar, and the two of them bounded out the door. With no time to spare, they ran straight to Park View Cemetery.

Chapter Twenty Six

Once inside the gates, Jake and Chrissy slowed to a brisk walk. They traveled around the winding path and up the hillside to the old section of the cemetery. Jake scanned the ground as they went, but there was no sign of the spy camera anywhere. When they finally reached the Stine Mausoleum, Jake looked around and made sure that he and Chrissy were alone.

"You stay here, girl," he said, letting go of her leash. He didn't need to secure it. She would never run off and leave him.

Chrissy sat down and cocked her head to the side.

"It's okay...I'll be right back," Jake said and rubbed her nose. Then he went to the large double doors and looked around again to see if anyone was watching. The coast was clear.

Slowly, Jake pushed the doors inward, allowing sunlight to barge into the house of tombs like an unwelcome guest. Even in the daylight, the place looked creepy, Jake thought. He stopped and listened for the whispering that he had heard the night before, but there was only silence. He stepped inside and noticed several sets of footprints that were larger than his and Leo's prints, and he followed them across the room. One of the prints seemed to disappear into the wall with the lions heads- the same wall where Leo had seen the witch come through. There was only a heel mark and nothing else. Where was the rest of that footprint? Jake wondered.

As he stared at the wall, he saw that one of the lions' heads was a little crooked, and he reached up and straightened it. Suddenly, part of the wall moved forward, startling him. He flinched, lurching backwards. Then, cautiously, he leaned forward and peered through the opening...

Chapter Twenty Seven

Jake saw a small dark room- a secret chamber. The other half of the footprint was just inside the door, and there was garbage and fake purple flowers next to a pillow and a rolled up sleeping bag. In the far corner, there was an unzipped duffel bag with a black wig and some black fabric laying on top. Did it belong to the woman in black? He wondered. Was she living there? He moved toward the bag, wanting to get a closer look...then suddenly he heard Chrissy barking.

Jake rushed out of the room and pushed the door shut. He hurried out of the mausoleum and saw Chrissy standing at full attention, her ears pointing upward as she stared intensely at something straight ahead.

"What is it, girl?" Jake asked, looking in the same direction.

He spotted a black cat sitting on a nearby tombstone, licking its paw. It was wearing a light blue collar with a silver heart tag, just like the one he had seen at Ava's house. Chrissy angled her ears back, which meant that she was nervous. Knowing that, Jake petted her head and wondered why she was behaving so strangely. She had never acted like that around Duke. She usually loved cats.

Just then, the cat stopped licking and looked right at them. It meowed loudly and leapt from its perch. In an instant, Chrissy took off running, her leash flapping behind her as she chased the cat down the hill and away from the mausoleum. Jake ran after her, screaming for her to stop.

Finally, Chrissy came to a halt by the walking path, allowing Jake to catch up to her. "What's gotten into you today?" He said, grabbing her leash. He looked around for the black cat, but it was gone. "We better get home."

As Jake turned to leave, he looked back at the old section of the cemetery and thought that he caught a glimpse of someone near the Stine Mausoleum. He stopped and did a double take, but no one was there. *It was probably just my imagination,* he told himself, staring up the hill. But his gut told him otherwise. Suddenly, he felt glad that the black cat had shown up when he did. It might have been a stroke of good luck, he thought.

Chapter Twenty Eight

Later, sitting between his parents in a pew at St. Jude's Church, Jake thought about the strange events of that morning- the secret chamber, the black cat and the mysterious figure near the mausoleum. What was going on at Park View Cemetery? He wondered. And how did it involve the woman in black? If only he had found his spy camera.

Jake glanced around the crowded church. He knew that Ava wouldn't be there. He had never once in his life seen her at St. Jude's. Mr. Pantloni had stopped going to church years ago, after his wife died. But Jake saw plenty of other familiar faces.

AJ was two rows in front of him, sitting with his family, and Cuss was off to the side with the rest of the choir. Leo and Reilly were in a pew with their parents several rows back on the other side of the aisle. Leo's head was lowered, which was a sure sign that he was napping, while Reilly appeared to be listening intently to Reverend Cusson's sermon on spreading joy.

Jake peered over his shoulder and saw Mariah Nightingale and her mom in their usual seats in the back row. With the same youthful fair skin and shoulder-length red hair, they looked more like sisters than mother and daughter. Jake watched as Bettina Nightingale smiled at her daughter and squeezed her arm affectionately. Just then, Mariah locked eyes with Jake. She had caught him looking at her. Embarrassed, he faced perfectly forward but felt her eyes upon him.

When it was finally time to leave, he rose with the rest of the congregation and glanced back in her direction, but their pew was empty. As he exited the church, however, he saw Mariah waiting near the bottom of the steps. Her mom was a few feet away, talking to another woman. Still feeling awkward that she had caught him looking at them, Jake tried to avoid eye contact, but soon it became clear that she was waiting for him.

"Can you meet me at the library in about 30 minutes?" She asked him, her tone rather serious.

"Sure," Jake said, surprised by her request.

As Mariah darted away, walking towards her mom, Jake couldn't help but notice that Bettina Nightingale was slim and average height...just like the woman in black.

Chapter Twenty Nine

Since Jake had thirty minutes before he had to meet up with Mariah, he decided to go to Brumbaugh's Bookstore to talk to Izzy again. He wanted to hear more stories about Lucinda Storm and the mysterious black cat, and he also wanted to tell Izzy the truth about *The Witching Hour* and what was happening to Ava. Maybe if Izzy knew what was really going on, she could help him piece things together.

When Jake approached Brumbaugh's, however, he saw that the store was closed.

Disappointed, he turned to leave and spotted Reilly and Dustin a few blocks up the street.

They were standing by themselves, talking and laughing. He had just seen Reilly at church, so she must have hurried to meet with Dustin right afterward. Jake's heart sank, and he started walking in the other direction, heading straight for the library. Although he would get there a good twenty minutes before Mariah, he didn't care. He just wanted to be as far away from Reilly and Dustin as possible.

A few minutes later, he entered the library and was surprised how busy it was for a Sunday afternoon. Mrs. Foley was standing behind her desk, stamping "date due" cards and placing them in a pile. Jake smiled and said hello, and she responded with a tight grin that looked more like a grimace. Obviously, she had missed Reverend Cusson's sermon on spreading joy, he thought.

He killed time wandering through aisles close to the door, pretending to look for books, while he thought about Reilly and Dustin's relationship and Ava's curse- two things that made no sense to him. As he lingered near the periodical section, he heard someone whisper his name.

Chapter Thirty

Jake turned around and saw Reilly standing there.

"Hi," she smiled. "What are you doing here on a Sunday afternoon? I thought you'd be home watching football."

"I'm meeting up with someone," Jake said, flatly. There was no need to give her any more details than that, he thought. Reilly obviously didn't care. She was too busy spending time with Dustin Kelly. "How about you?" He asked.

"Oh, I followed you from Main Street," she said. Then her face reddened and she smiled nervously. "I mean, I saw you, and I wanted to tell you how much I liked the book."

"The book?" He asked. "Oh, *The Hound of the Baskervilles*."

"Yeah, I just finished it," she said. "It was so good...just like you said."

Jake couldn't help but smile. "I'm glad you liked it."

"I *loved* it," she said. "It definitely kept me guessing." There was an awkward pause in their conversation. "Well, I hope everything's okay with Ava," she said. "Tell her I said hi."

"I will," Jake nodded. "And tell Dustin Kelley that I said hi."

Reilly gave him a curious look. "What do you mean?" She asked.

"I don't know," Jake replied, shrugging his shoulders. "I saw you two on Main Street earlier and at Al's the other day, so I guess I just thought..."

"Oh my gosh," Reilly laughed, interrupted him. "I forgot my ballet slippers at dance class yesterday and went to get them after church." She patted the tote bag hanging over her shoulder. "That's when I saw Dustin on Main Street. We talked about ballet. He's been taking dance classes with me to help him jump higher in football. It was the coach's suggestion, and Dustin asked me not to broadcast it. I think he's a little embarrassed about it." She dug a small card out of her purse and handed it to Jake. "He even gave me this thank you note." The card read:

Dear Reilly,

You're a good friend. Thanks for your help.

Dustin.

"See. We're just friends," she said. "He's a really nice guy, and I hope things work out for him and Ava. I know he still likes her."

Jake looked at the card and noticed that it was the same writing that was on the note that Ava had found in her locker. On the back of the card was a dark smudge that came off easily onto his finger, just like the smudge he had found on Ava's note.

Chapter Thirty One

"It's that stuff that you guys wear around your eyes to block the sun when you're playing sports," Reilly said, seeing him notice the smudge. "What's it called? Black Eye?"

Jake laughed. "You mean Eye Black," he said.

"Shhh!" Mrs. Foley scolded them.

They moved down the aisle, farther away from Mrs. Foley's desk. "Well, it really makes a mess," Reilly giggled, quietly.

"Do you mind if I keep this for a couple of days?" Jake asked, holding up the card. "I'll give it back. I promise." He wanted to show Ava the note, so that she could see for herself that the note had been from Dustin, wanting to meet up with her, and not from the woman in black.

At that moment, Mariah entered the library, and Jake waved in her direction. "She wants to talk to me about something," he explained before Reilly could ask.

Reilly grinned. "I better be getting home anyway," she said.

Jake smiled and said goodbye, happy to have seen her and know the truth about her and Dustin. Then Reilly and Mariah exchanged quick hellos, as they passed each other.

"Shhh!" Mrs. Foley said again.

“Come on,” Jake whispered to Mariah, as she approached him. “Let’s go to the zoo room.” He knew they had a lot to talk about, and he was growing tired of getting shushed.

Although the zoo room was crowded, they managed to find two seats in the far corner.

“I’m sorry I was rude to you on the phone yesterday,” Mariah said right away, her large blue eyes cast downward.

Jake smiled. “That’s okay. I must have sounded pretty crazy.”

“Not really,” she said. “I shouldn’t have bought that book...especially since that guy reserved it for someone else.”

“Wait...” Jake look surprised. “So, you *do* have *The Witching Hour*?”

Mariah leaned down and retrieved a thick, black, hardcover book from her tote bag on the floor and then placed it on the table in front of Jake. Carefully, he picked it up with both hands. Jake couldn’t believe it. He finally had *The Witching Hour*.

Chapter Thirty Two

"I bought it for my mom," Mariah said. "Anne Rice is her favorite author. Ever since my dad died, she reads all the time." There was a hint of sadness in her voice.

"But she already finished reading it, so when I told her what happened, she said that I should give it to you."

"Thanks," Jake said. "That was really nice of her...and you. And I'm really sorry about your dad."

Mariah shrugged her shoulders. "It's been about three years now, so I guess my mom and I are doing okay. But I wish she didn't have to work so much." Mariah told him that her mom had been working two jobs- a nursing job at the hospital and waiting tables at a local Italian restaurant called Lena's.

Jake felt bad for Mariah. "It must be hard being by yourself a lot," he said. "You can always come over to my house for dinner, although my mom makes a lot of things that my dad and I have to pretend to like."

Mariah laughed. "Maybe I will," she said.

Jake opened the cover of the book and saw a bright yellow post-it note stuck to the title page. It read: **Save for R.S**.

"Oh, I forgot to throw that out," Mariah said, noticing Jake looking at the note. "Some guy at Brumbaugh's picked up *The Witching Hour* before I did, and I thought he was going to buy it, but he just carried it around for a few seconds and then stuck that post-it on the cover and put the book on the RESERVED cart."

"So, that's what you meant when you said you shouldn't have bought it?" Jake asked.

"Yeah, I felt bad afterwards. Is R.S the woman who owned the book?"

"Maybe," Jake said, thinking that it had to be Rachel Storm, Lucinda Storm's niece. But why wouldn't the man just buy it for her? He wondered. "Do you remember what the guy looked like?" He asked.

"I only really saw him from the back," Mariah said. "But I remember that he was wearing a camouflage coat and a knit hat and was kind of big and tall."

Coach Phillips was big and tall, Jake thought. He asked Mariah if that's who she had seen.

She furrowed her brow. "I don't know...maybe. I'm not in any of his classes, so I've never really gotten a good look at him. Plus, this guy acted really strangely. I saw him take some flowers from a vase in the store before he left. I can't imagine a teacher doing something like that. It was really weird."

"Were they purple?" Jake asked, thinking about the flowers he had seen in the Stine Mausoleum.

"Yeah." Mariah looked surprised. "How'd you know?"

"Lucky guess," Jake said.

Mariah grinned. "Well, I better be going," she said, rising to her feet. "My mom is waiting outside in the car."

Jake stood up, too, and fished money out of his pocket. "Here, let me pay you for the book," he said, holding out a ten dollar bill.

Mariah waved her hand in protest. "That's okay. I just hope it all works out."

After she left, Jake sat back down and flipped through the pages of *The Witching Hour*, searching for any sort of clue to explain the book's importance or value. There was no inscription by the author, and it wasn't a first edition. Plus, the binding looked a little damaged, so it couldn't be worth much, he thought. He removed the dust jacket and inspected it carefully but found nothing.

Frustrated, he sighed and turned the book over. Then something caught his eye.

There was something hidden in the spine of *The Witching Hour.*

Chapter Thirty Three

Jake could see the metal tip of an object wedged tightly between the pages. Using his finger, he tried to fish it out but only managed to push it down deeper. Determined, he changed his strategy and pressed his thumb against the outside of the spine until he felt the object. Then, slowly, he pushed up from the bottom until a small brass key emerged from the book and tumbled onto the table. With the number 222 engraved beneath the keyhole, it looked like a key to a safe deposit box. A smile formed on Jake's face. He had found what he was looking for...and he knew what he had to do next.

Ten minutes later, he arrived at Splinters Bowling Alley. He noticed that the parking lot looked a little more crowded than usual. Maybe business was finally improving, he thought. He started to go inside, when he spotted a dark van enter the lot and disappear around the side of the building. Curious, he ran over to check it out. He peeked around the corner and stared down the same alley where Ava had said she had seen Coach Phillips arguing with a man about money.

The van was backed up to the side doors of the bowling alley. Three men wearing dark suits and sunglasses were busy unloading black cases and carrying them inside of the building. Jake didn't recognize any of them, but he listened as they joked about making easy money.

Finally, when all three of them were inside of the building, Jake knew what he had to do. He sprinted over to the van and quickly looked inside the doors. There was one black case, slightly larger than a briefcase, still in the back. He reached his hand out to open it.

"You caught me," said a sudden voice from behind.

Startled, Jake twisted around to see Coach Phillips smiling at him.

"I don't know anything." Jake blurted out, his arms up in surrender.

"Relax, Jake," Coach Phillips laughed. "I'm just joking around. I guess it was only a matter of time before people from school heard about all of this." Wearing the same kind of suit as the other men, he adjusted his jacket. Then he reached into his pocket and pulled out a small ceramic cat. It looked just like the one that Ava had found in her locker. Jake couldn't help but stare at it, and Coach Phillips noticed. "Oh, it's just a little gift from my girlfriend," he said, looking amused. "For good luck."

Panicked, Jake took a step backward, getting ready to bolt...

Chapter Thirty Four

"Don't look so scared, kid," Coach Phillips said. "We sound pretty good for a bunch of old guys. And we even play some of our own songs."

Suddenly, Jake was confused. "Wait...you're in a band?" He asked.

"Yeah, The Blue Dogs," Coach Phillips replied. "Why? Did you think I was a solo act?"

"No...It's just...I mean...Ava saw you here arguing about money and thought..."

"Oh, yeah," the coach interrupted. "I saw her in the alley that day and noticed that she looked upset, but I was too busy arguing to ask her if she was okay. You see, the other guys in the band wanted more money for this gig, but my girlfriend, Rachel, who owns the place, is on kind of a tight budget right now. But that'll change when the word spreads about us."

"So that's what you were yelling about on the phone after practice yesterday?" Jake asked.

Coach Phillips nodded. Then one of the suited men appeared in the doorway.

"We're all set up, Chip, but we need you for a sound check."

Jake knew that the coach's first name was Charles, but he'd never heard him called Chip before. He was learning a lot about Coach Phillips.

"Thanks, Nick," the coach said. "Come on, Jake." He grabbed the black case and shut the van door. "You can meet the rest of the guys."

Jake hesitated for a second. Then he secured *The Witching Hour* under his arm and followed the coach through the side doors of Splinters. As soon as he saw The Blue Dogs with their instruments, he breathed a sigh of relief. Coach Phillips had been telling the truth. He really *was* in a band. But what about Rachel Storm? He wondered. And the ceramic cat? And the key in the spine of The Witching Hour? Maybe Coach Phillips was dating the woman in black and he didn't even know it...or maybe she had tricked him into helping her. There were still so many unanswered questions.

Jake met the rest of the band and stood back as they started to play. He couldn't believe how good they sounded. Lead singer, Coach Phillips, looked surprisingly cool, belting out the notes like a pro, while the rest of the guys played their instruments and danced behind him. Jake was impressed, and he looked around to see if everyone else was, too. That's when he spotted Rachel Storm standing behind the busy concession counter. Jake recognized her face from the newspaper. He went over to meet her.

Chapter Thirty Five

As Jake waited in the concession line, he made three observations about Rachel Storm: she was prettier than her picture, seemed nicer than he expected and was about the same size as the woman in black. Finally, it was his turn.

"What can I get for you?" She smiled at Jake.

"I'll have a Coke, please," he said, setting *The Witching Hour* on the counter, which he saw her notice right away.

"I like a guy who brings a book to a bowling alley," she joked, as she filled up his cup. "You must be a smart kid."

Jake smiled. "Actually, it belongs to my friend, Ava. She bought it from Brumbaugh's Bookstore recently. But I think it used to belong to your Aunt Lucinda."

"Really?" She said, sounding pleasantly surprised. She set the drink in front of him and stared at the book on the counter. "What a cool coincidence."

"Well, to be honest, it's not really a coincidence," Jake said, as he laid his money on the counter. "I brought it here because I was hoping that you could help me."

He quickly introduced himself and told her about Ava and the woman in black.

Then he laid the key next to the book. "I found this key in the book," he said. "I thought that maybe it belonged to your aunt and that you were trying to get it back."

Rachel's eyes widened. She looked genuinely surprised. "No, I've honestly never seen this before," she said, picking up the key to examine it. "It looks like a key to a safe deposit box or something like that, but my Aunt Lucinda didn't have a lot of money or valuables, except the things she left me when she died."

"What about the ceramic cat?" Jake asked, politely. "Ava found one in her locker, and I saw that Coach Phillips had one just like it. He said that you had given it to him."

Rachel gestured for one of her employees to take over and then she and Jake moved to the end of the counter. "You must be talking about Ava Pantloni," she whispered, excitedly. "I haven't seen her in so long..."

Chapter Thirty Six

"Ava's mom was a dear friend of my Aunt Lucinda's," Rachel explained. "I even babysat Ava a few times when I was a teenager visiting my aunt, and she was just an infant, but I haven't seen her since her mom passed away. So, when Chip, I mean Coach Phillips, told me that he saw her crying, I asked him to put the cat figurine in her locker. It's just a good luck charm that belonged to my aunt."

"Wow." Jake was astonished. "I had no idea...and Ava will be so surprised. She thought it was some kind of symbol that she was cursed or something."

"Oh, I'm so sorry," she said, sincerely. "I feel terrible. I was just trying to help. And my Aunt Lucinda was the nicest woman. She had severe arthritis for most of her life and couldn't really leave the house. I guess that's why people were scared of her- because she was different and kept to herself. But she had a kind heart and never hurt a soul."

"Do you really think it's possible that she could come back? Maybe even as a cat?"

Rachel grinned. "Well, my aunt definitely believed in the power of magic," she said. "And she taught me that as long as you truly believe in magic, anything is possible."

She gave him a wink. “Now, I *believe* I have to get back to work,” she joked. “But it was very nice meeting you, Jacob Finn.”

“Nice meeting you, too, Miss Storm,” he said. “And please call me Jake. All my friends do.”

“Will do,” she smiled. “But only if you call me Rachel.”

Jake agreed and thanked her for her help. He liked Rachel Storm and was glad to have been wrong about her and Coach Phillips, even though he was disappointed that he still hadn’t solved the mystery.

As Jake walked home in the light rain, he tried to make sense of all of the clues he had found but just couldn’t piece them all together. Soon the rain came down harder and despite his loafers and dress clothes, Jake started to jog. With *The Witching Hour* secured tightly against his chest, he began to run, picking up speed as he neared his house. He felt fast and strong, as the cold water slapped against his face. Running was one of his all- time favorite things to do. It always cleared his head.

For a few minutes, Jake had forgotten all about Ava and the woman in black and just focused on speed. He felt exhilarated. He was so caught up in the joy of running that he didn’t even notice that a black car was following him.

Chapter Thirty Seven

With one huge leap, Jake flew onto the porch, almost smacking into his dad, who had managed to jump out of the way just in the nick of time.

"Holy heck, Jake!" Sam Finn exclaimed, his back against the front door.

"I'm so sorry, Dad," Jake said, breathlessly. "Are you okay?"

Before his dad could answer, Jake's mom opened the door, and Sam Finn nearly fell backwards.

"Oh, dear!" she said, as Sam struggled to regain his balance.

"Geez! Are you both trying to kill me?!" He joked, making them laugh.

"We're going grocery shopping and have a few other errands, if you want to come with us, Jake," his mom said. "I didn't know if you'd be back in time, so I left you a note on the counter."

"No, that's okay." Jake shook his head. "I have homework to do."

"Well, there's meatloaf in the fridge, and we have our cell phones in case of an emergency." His mom kissed him on the cheek. "And the Holloways are home, if you need them, but don't go over there unless something's wrong because Chrissy doesn't like being left in a storm. And don't ask Leo to come over unless your homework is done. And lock the front door and don't open it for anyone except Leo."

"Okay, okay," Jake replied to his mom's familiar speech.

"Be back soon! Love you!" She hollered, hurrying to the car with her arm over her head to shield herself from the rain.

Jake stood in the doorway and waved, as his parents drove away. Before he closed the door, however, he noticed a black car with tinted windows parked across the street.

The engine was running, and Jake had a feeling that there was someone in the car, watching him. Was it the woman in black? He wondered. Did she know that he had *The Witching Hour*? And the key?

Jake shook off his fears. It was just someone picking up a neighbor or using their cell phone, he told himself, shutting the door and locking it. He laid the book and the key on the foyer table and went to the back door and did the same. When he returned to the front of the house, he peeked out the window again...

Chapter Thirty Eight

He saw that the black car was gone. Relieved and hungry, Jake went to the kitchen and made himself a thick meatloaf sandwich. He gobbled it down fast, anxious to get started on his homework, so he could finish and see Leo. As he took his last bite, there was a loud rumble of thunder then a flash of lightning, and Chrissy wimpered.

"It's okay, girl." Jake petted her head. Then he grabbed the key and *The Witching Hour* and went upstairs with Chrissy following closely behind him. When he opened the door to his bedroom, he saw Duke hiding under the bed, his eyes as big as saucers.

"You're safe there, Duke," Jake laughed. He settled at his desk and went straight to work, reading the ten assigned pages of *Macbeth* and then finishing his algebra. Just as he laid down his pencil, his walkie talkie crackled.

"Jake, are you there?" It was Leo's voice.

Jake picked it up and pushed in the button. "Yep. Perfect timing," he said. "I just finished my homework. Can you come over? I have so much to tell you."

"Okay. I'll be there in fifteen," Leo replied before signing off.

When he showed up, the boys went right to the family room. There, they watched a little football on TV while

Jake filled Leo in on everything that had happened that day, including finding the key in the spine of *The Witching Hour*.

"I definitely think it's a key to a safe deposit box... because of the numbers," Leo said, holding it up to examine it. "I've seen a lot of them on detective shows."

Jake nodded. He had thought the same thing about the key. "But if the guy that Mariah saw knew that they key was in there, why didn't he just buy the book? Why did he leave it for R.S.?"

"Maybe the guy didn't have any cash on him," Leo said. "That happens to me all the time."

Just then Jake saw a Channel 10 News Update appear on the TV screen. It showed the surveillance video of Michael Pratt when he had robbed the bank. He had been wearing black clothes and a scary mask and black wig. It was the first time that Jake had seen that footage. Then Channel 10 aired "recently obtained" video taken at the bus station shortly after the robbery. It showed Michael Pratt dressed in regular clothes and boarding the 3:10 PM bus headed out of town. The reporter said that police believed that the bus station video proved that Michael Pratt had managed to skip town.

Jake stared at the images on TV. "You're brilliant, Leo!" Jake exclaimed.

"Yeah, I know," Leo said. "But why do you think so?"

Jake smiled. "Because you were right about the guy not having the cash on him," he said. "But that's not why he didn't buy the book."

Chapter Thirty Nine

Jake had figured out most of the mystery. He explained to Leo that Michael Pratt couldn't have left town at 3:10 the day of the robbery like the police thought. In the video from the bus station, Michael Pratt was wearing a camouflage coat and knit hat, just like the man who Mariah had seen at 3:30 that same afternoon, which means that he had only pretended to leave town.

Leo gave him a funny look. "But why would he hang out in the bookstore when the police were after him?"

"He needed a place to stash the key, just in case the police stopped him," Jake said. "You know the lockers that were behind the reporter at the bus station? I think that's where Michael Pratt stashed the stolen money."

Leo's face lit up. "In locker 222!"

"Yep," Jake said. "Then he hid the key in the first book he saw and left it for his accomplice to buy."

"R.S.," Leo said.

"Exactly. Then he headed for the cemetery to hide out in the Stine Mausoleum."

"Oh, that's why he stole the flowers!" Leo shouted. "So he wouldn't look suspicious, just in case someone saw him in the cemetery!"

Jake nodded. "He must have called R.S. and told her where the key was hidden so she could buy the book, get the key, and use it to get the stolen money. Then they would meet up and leave town."

"But Mariah bought the book before she could get it," Leo added.

"And the woman in black thought it was Ava," Jake said. "So, R.S. has to be the woman in black..." Suddenly, Jake sprang to his feet and rushed to the kitchen.

"What is it?!" Leo asked, quickly following behind him. The key was still in his hand.

"I have to warn Ava," Jake said, picking up the phone. "If Michael Pratt and his accomplice really believe that Ava has the key to their money, then this is more serious than some silly curse. She could be in real danger."

Jake dialed her number from memory, but it went straight to voicemail. He listened to her cheerful pre-recorded message and waited for the beep.

"Hi, Ava. It's Jake," he said. "It's really important that you call me right away. It's about *The Witching Hour*." Jake pushed the end button. He started to dial another number but stopped before he had finished.

"Who are you calling now?" Leo asked.

"The Michael Pratt hotline number. But I can't remember it."

Leo grabbed the newspaper off the kitchen counter. "Here it is," he said, pointing to the bottom of the front page. "But I don't think you should call. You're a kid, so no one's going to take you seriously."

"We don't have a choice. We have to report what we know."

"You're right," Leo said. Then he smiled mischievously. "I have an idea."

Chapter Forty

Doing his finest "Mr. Twiddy" impersonation, Leo left the following message on the hotline number:

"Hi. This is Stanley Twiddy. I'm a bus driver for Grove City School District and have been doing that for about thirty years, which means I've been carting around a bunch of worthless kids for most of my life. Anywho, I have some information about that knucklehead Michael Pratt. I was power walking in Park View Cemetery today, trying to get fit for Mrs. Twiddy, when I spotted him going into the Stine Mausoleum. So, maybe you should get off your big keisters and go arrest him before he gets away from you again."

It was perfect- the voice, the insults- it sounded just like Mr. Twiddy, and Jake couldn't help but laugh, despite his concern for Ava. "That was your best work yet," he said to Leo.

"Thanks. I've been practicing," Leo replied. "I just hope that someone gets the message soon. It freaks me out to think that there's a couple of crazies on the loose."

Jake told Leo about the black car that had been parked across the street, and Leo suddenly looked panicked. He stared at the key that he had set on the kitchen counter.

"That means that they know that *you* have the key!" He exclaimed. "Oh, my gosh! *You're* in danger! *We're* in danger!"

"Geez, Leo...settle down," Jake said, calmly. "My parents are going to be home any minute, and I'll tell them what's going on. They'll call the police, and everything will be okay. You'll see. No one is going to get hurt." It was wishful thinking, and Jake knew it.

A few seconds later, Jake heard the sound of a car engine, and he raced to the family room. He expected to see his parents' car pulling into the driveway. Instead, when he looked out the window, he saw that the black car was back...and moving slowly past his house. His heart began to race.

"What is it?!" Leo asked, urgently, standing behind him. He looked over Jake's shoulder just as the car turned out of sight. Then an angry bolt of lightning lit up the sky. "Geez! That was fierce," Leo said.

"Yeah," Jake agreed. He was glad that Leo hadn't seen the car. It was better that way, he thought. Suddenly, the phone rang, and both boys jumped with surprise.

"I hope the police didn't trace our call," Leo said, as Jake rushed to get the phone.

Jake looked at the Caller ID. It was Ava's number. Thank goodness, he thought, picking it up. With no time for hellos, he got right to the point.

"Ava, you're in danger," he spoke fast. "I have *The Witching Hour*, but Michael Pratt and the woman in black are trying to get it, and they might think that you have it, so you have to tell your dad what's going on and have him call the police." Jake stopped and took a breath while he waited for her response. But there was only silence. "Ava? Are you there?" He asked.

"I want my book," said a woman's voice.

A chill went down Jake's spine. "Where's Ava?" He said.

"Oh, she's with me," she sneered. "The bench by the angel statue in Park View Cemetery. Leave it there by midnight tonight or else you won't see your little friend again." Her voice was cold and raspy, like a wicked witch in a fairy tale. "And don't do anything stupid like call the police. That'll only make things worse for her...and for you."

"I want to talk to Ava," Jake said, trying to sound braver than he felt. "For all I know you just stole her phone."

There was a brief pause and then Ava came on the line.

"Jake, please help me!" She cried.

"Is that proof enough for you?" The woman asked. "Now, give me my book, and I'll give you your friend."

Before he could respond, he heard another phone ring, and then the line went dead.

Chapter Forty One

A few minutes later, Jake and Leo were on their way to Park View Cemetery...again.

It was getting dark outside. The thunder and lightning had stopped, but the rain was still coming down hard, and their windbreakers were already drenched. Jake had returned the key to the spine of *The Witching Hour* and had put the book in a Ziplock bag to keep it from getting wet. Then he had tucked it under his arm. It was still securely in place when the boys reached the familiar wrought iron gates.

"We should have told our parents or Ava's dad," Leo said, as they entered the cemetery.

"Ava's dad is out of town, and our parents would have called the police, and that could have been bad for Ava."

"Well, this could be bad for us," Leo griped. "What if they don't let her go? What if she's not even up here?"

As they stepped onto the path, Jake heard the sound of a car engine. He turned around and spotted a black car in front of the gate. His pulse quickened. "Let's just do this as fast as we can," he said, picking up the pace.

Soon they had wound their way around the path and were stepping onto the hill toward the old section of Park View. The grass was rain-soaked and slippery, and Jake almost lost his footing. He was distracted, thinking about the black car. Had it followed them there? He wondered.

The boys kept going, quieter than they had ever been in their lives and staying close together as they wove through the wet tombstones. When they neared the bench, Jake heard a rustling noise behind him. He stopped and looked around.

"What is it?" Leo whispered, nervously.

"I thought I heard something, but I guess it was just the rain."

Then, suddenly, out of the corner of his eye, Jake saw a large dark figure rushing towards them, closing in on them so fast that he couldn't even scream.

Chapter Forty Two

It was Michael Pratt. Jake could see his angry face, as he lunged toward him and Leo. In an instant, he had pushed Leo to the ground and had grabbed Jake's hood, twisting it violently in his hands. The boys seemed doomed until, suddenly, the black cat with the blue collar came out of nowhere, leaping onto Michael Pratt's back and causing him to scream out in pain. He lost his balance and fell to the wet grass. Then, in a flash, the cat was gone.

"Freeze!" Screamed a man, popping up from behind a nearby tombstone. He was wearing a long gray trench coat and aiming a gun directly at Michael Pratt.

"Don't move!" Said another voice. It was a woman, also wearing a trench coat, standing near the man in gray. She came out from behind a different tombstone and swiftly handcuffed Michael Pratt. Then two other men in trench coats appeared on the scene, pulling Michael Pratt to his feet. Soon, they had escorted him away from the area.

That's when Jake noticed his spy camera on the ground where Michael Pratt had been laying. He pointed it out to Leo, and they both went over to get it.

"I'm Detective Bardell," said the man in the gray trench coat, walking toward them with the woman who had handcuffed Michael Pratt. "This is my partner, Detective Ling. Do you mind telling us what you kids are doing here? You know, you could have been hurt."

"We know, Sir," Jake said. "But our friend, Ava Pantloni, was kidnapped by a woman who was helping Michael Pratt."

Detective Bardell looked confused. "Wait a second," he said, putting his hands up, as if to stop them. "Ava Pantloni? Prosecutor Edward Pantloni's daughter?"

Jake and Leo both nodded.

"You're saying she's been kidnapped?"

'Yep, that's pretty much what we're saying," Leo replied.

"We weren't supposed to tell anyone," Jake said, "especially the police, but now that Michael Pratt has been arrested...could you just please hurry and check the Stine Mausoleum. There's a secret room in there, and I think that's where she's being held."

"We already found that room," Detective Ling said. "We had a phone tip a little while ago that Pratt was in there."

Leo looked at Jake and mouthed the words *Mr. Twiddy.*

"And Ava wasn't there?" Jake asked in disbelief.

"Sorry," Detective Ling said, shaking her head. "We didn't even find the stolen money...just some bedding and clothes, including his costume and a lot of garbage." She pointed to a nearby garbage can, piled high with trash.

"Oh, we know where the mon..."

"So all of that garbage is from the Stine Mausoleum?" Jake interrupted Leo. He noticed that all of the take-out containers in the trash can were from the same restaurant.

"Yes, it is," Detective Bardell said. "The guy was a real slob. It looked like the bottom of a birdcage in there."

Jake's eyes lit up. "That's it!" He said to Leo. Then he turned to the detectives. "I know where Ava is!" He exclaimed. "And I think I know who kidnapped her!"

Chapter Forty Three

Jake told the detectives that Ava was being held in the storage room of Brumbaugh's Bookstore. The ringing sound on the phone had been Jasper, and the food wrappers from The Doughnut Hole were there because Becca was Michael Pratt's accomplice. Her real name was probably Rebecca. She had to be R.S.

Jake handed Detective Bardell the key to the bus locker and told him where the money was, and that Michael Pratt had probably wanted to leave on the bus that day but had to change his plans when the teller had identified him.

"So he stashed the money in locker 222," Jake said. "And left the key for Becca since she could easily go to the bus terminal and get the money without anyone thinking twice about it. Then he stole the flowers from the bookstore and walked through the cemetery looking like someone visiting a grave and not drawing any attention to himself. It was a good plan. But by the time he called Becca to tell her that the key was in the spine of *The Witching Hour*, the book was already gone."

"And that Frank guy messed up big time," Leo said. "Because when Becca pretended that some angry woman had come into the book store looking for *The Witching*

Hour, he told her that it was Ava Pantloni who had the book, when it was really Mariah Nightingale. And there's this crazy cat on the loose," Leo continued. "Maybe you saw it. It's black and wears a blue collar and was attacking Michael Pratt..."

"I think we've heard enough," Detective Bardell interrupted.

"But we're telling the truth!" Jake pleaded.

"We believe you," Detective Ling said. "Now, let's get you boys home safely so we can go rescue your friend."

Chapter Forty Four

That night, Jake laid in bed, thinking about the day's events. Michael Pratt and Rebecca Stine had been arrested, the stolen money had been found in bus locker 222, like Jake had thought, and Ava was home safe and sound, after being held in the storage room of Brumbaugh's Bookstore for several hours. According to Mr. Pantloni, who had rushed back from his business trip and had called Jake's dad earlier that evening, Ava was in perfect health, except for a severe ear infection, which had explained her dizziness that week.

Jake and his parents had learned from the police that Rebecca "Becca" Stine was from a middle class family, distantly related to the wealthier Stine family, who had built the mausoleum. As a child, she had heard the stories of the hidden chamber and had shared the information with her secret boyfriend, Michael Pratt. Police had also told them that they had found Becca's disguise in her apartment, along with fake IDs and two airline tickets for a Sunday morning flight out of the country, which had explained the Saturday night deadline for getting the key.

Channel 10 had reported that evening that Michael Pratt had admitted to coming out of hiding several times that week and borrowing Becca's car to help him search for the missing key. Jake thought about the break-in attempt at Ava's house, and the black car that had been parked outside of his own house. Apparently, Michael Pratt had looked up Ava's address and had found Jake's address on the side of the spy camera.

Jake took a deep breath. Thankfully, things had ended well. He and Leo hadn't even gotten in trouble for leaving the house without permission. Their parents had been so proud of their heroism that a strongly worded safety lecture had been their only punishment.

Jake looked across the room at his copy of The Hound of The Baskervilles on the top shelf of his bookcase. He thought about the similarities between his favorite book and Ava's mystery- the curse, the robber hiding on the moors and the ghostly dog on the loose. In Jake's case, it had been a robber in a cemetery and a ghostly cat, but it still made him think of it. Of course, at the end of The Hound of the Baskervilles, Sherlock Holmes solved the case using logic and sound reasoning. There were no unanswered questions.

But with Ava's mystery, there were still a missing piece to the puzzle...and he couldn't stop thinking about it.

Chapter Forty Five

Suddenly, Jake heard a quiet tapping on his door. He knew it was his dad. His mom had already come in and hugged him three times that night, telling him how much she loved him and how proud she was of him. Sometimes, Jake thought that he was too old for all that lovey dovey stuff, but he didn't feel that way tonight.

"Come in," he said, sitting up.

"Hey, champ," his dad smiled. "Just making sure you haven't escaped out the window," he joked.

"Nope," Jake laughed. "But thanks for not grounding me."

"That's kind of what I wanted to talk to you about."

Jake sighed. "Okay, well I guess I have it coming.... breaking the rules and telling a few white lies, but I just really like helping people."

Sam tousled Jake's hair. "I get it," he said. "But you need to tell us what's going on from now on. We're a family...a team. Okay?"

"Okay," Jake nodded. He paused for a second. "Dad, can I ask you a question?"

"Sure," he said.

"Do you believe in witchcraft? Like someone being able to turn themselves into a cat?"

Sam Finn laughed.

"I'm serious," Jake said. "There was a black cat in that cemetery, and it saved our lives...more than once, and part of me thinks that it was some kind of magic."

"Well, when you put it like that, I'd have to say yes," his dad said. "Because I definitely believe in magic."

"You do?" Jake sounded surprised.

"Of course I do." Sam smiled. "I'm not sure about the whole cat thing, but the first time I held your mom's hand, I knew that there was such a thing as magic."

Jake grumbled. "Oh, geez...that's not what I meant."

His dad chuckled. "You'll understand one day. Now, get some sleep." He stood up and went to the door. "And Jake?" He said, turning around.

"I know...I'm grounded, right?"

"Nope," he said. "I just got off the phone with Mr. Pantloni for the second time tonight. He called back to thank you again for saving Ava's life and to thank us for raising such a great kid." He paused. "I love you, Jake. And I'm proud of you." Then he tossed something onto Jake's bed. "Your mom and I didn't go to the grocery store today, so I guess we told a little white lie, too."

Jake picked up the cell phone. "Are you serious?!" He exclaimed, smiling from ear to ear "This is the best surprise ever! Thank you so much, Dad!"

"You're welcome, pal," he said. "Maybe you can use it to call Mr. Twiddy and thank him for telling the police where Michael Pratt was hiding. Channel 10 just released his phone call to the hotline. Boy, I never realized what a mean, old goat he was, but he did save your hide. Now, get some sleep," he said, as he shut the door.

Jake's smile was gone. "Oh no," he mumbled to himself, pulling the sheet over his head. "We really are knuckleheads."

Chapter Forty Six

Two months later, a large group of people gathered at Splinters Bowling Alley for the church Christmas party. The mood was fun and lively, everyone talking and laughing as they bowled and listened to The Blue Dogs perform. Coach Phillips' band had become a huge local success and had helped make Splinters the new hot spot. Plus, Coach Phillips and Rachel Storm had recently gotten engaged, and Jake had never seen the coach look so happy.

As Jake stood in the concession line, waiting to get sodas for him and his friends, he thought about all of the other good things that had happened since that terrible day when Ava was kidnapped.

Michael Pratt and Rebecca Stine had both plead guilty and were serving long jail sentences. The prosecutor, Mr. Pantloni, had made sure of it.

Ava and her dad had grown close again and had even returned to the church.

That's where he had met Mariah's mom, and the two had been dating for several weeks.

Mr. Pantloni, who never used to smile, now smiled all of the time, and Ava and Mariah had become as close as sisters. Mariah even did all of the cheerleaders' hair before their games and competitions, replacing the one braid look with a new criss-cross braid that had become the hot new trend with the girls in school.

Ava and Dustin had gotten back together and were a great couple, although she had joked to Jake that Dustin wasn't allowed to leave notes in her locker anymore.

Izzy had hired a sweet, old lady to replace Becca at Brumbaugh's, and Frank was especially nice to Jake whenever he saw him, giving him a generous discount on anything he bought in the store.

Mr. Twiddy, having first denied to the police and the media that he had giving any sort of phone tip about Michael Pratt, eventually took credit for it, after learning about the cash reward. He and Mrs. Twiddy spent the money on a two week cruise to the Bahamas, and the grumpy, old bus driver had come back from their trip deeply tanned and a little less miserable.

As for Jake, things were going well. His grades were good, and he was having a lot of fun playing basketball that season and hanging out with Leo, AJ and Cuss off the court. He also loved having a cell phone, especially since Leo's parents had gotten Leo one, too. Jake had made it through the brief media storm that had occurred when word had leaked out about his role in finding Ava and the missing money, and he had taken Leo with him to every interview, always crediting his best buddy and a lot of luck for helping him solve the mystery.

"Hey, Jake," Rachel smiled, when it was his turn to order. "What can I get you?"

"A pitcher of Coke, please."

"Coming right up," she said. "By the way, I have something to show you." She took a picture out of her wallet and laid it on the counter in front of him. "That's my Aunt Lucinda."

Jake stared at the picture of a kind-looking woman wearing a light blue necklace with a silver heart...just like the collar on the black cat. He couldn't believe his eyes.

"I really miss her," Rachel said. "But I have a feeling that she's still with me, watching out for me. I think that she's happy that I'm getting married, and that I'm living here in Grove City, surrounded by such good people."

"I'm sure she is," Jake said. He looked around the bowling alley and saw his parents bowling with Mr. and Mrs. Holloway and AJ's mom and dad. One lane over, Gram and Pop had teamed up with Cuss's parents and Mr. Pantloni and Mariah's mom.

All of them smiling broadly and teasing each other good-naturedly. Leo, AJ and Cuss were in the far lane beside Mariah, Ava, Lexi and Ellis. The girls were high-fiving each other, celebrating Lexi's strike, while AJ and Leo roared with laughter, as Cuss slipped, shouting, "Sugar!" as he landed in the gutter. All the while, Coach Phillips was singing his heart out.

Yep, Jake thought. Rachel was definitely surrounded by good people.

He thanked her for the soda and went to rejoin the guys, still thinking about the picture. Had Lucinda Storm really come back as a cat? He wondered again. Had she saved him and Leo? Had she protected Ava from harm?

Just then, Jake spotted Reilly walking towards him. She was wearing a red sleeveless sweater, her hair in loose curls. Jake thought she looked prettier than ever.

"Want to bowl with me?" She smiled, rubbing her hands down her arms for warmth. "I'm so stupid for wearing this sweater. It's freezing in here, and I can't bowl in my heavy winter coat."

Jake set the pitcher of soda down on a nearby table. “Here,” he said, taking off his school jacket. “You can wear this.”

Reilly hesitated. “But don’t you need it?” She asked.

“No, I’m fine,” Jake said, holding it out for her. As she slid her arms into the leather sleeves, their hands briefly touched, and he forgot all about Lucinda Storm and the black cat. In that moment, Jake realized something amazing...that no matter what had happened at Park View Cemetery, his dad was right. There was such a thing as magic.

THE END

About the Author

Margaret S. Baker lives in Altoona, PA with her husband, Scott, and their son, Jake. After a successful career in pharmaceutical sales, she is now a full-time mom and writer.

CPSIA information can be obtained at www.ICGtesting.com
Printed in the USA
BVOW04s1846201016

465603BV00013B/128/P